Vincent Bijlo

The Institute

Translated by Susan Ridder

Holland Park Press London

Published by Holland Park Press 2017

Copyright © Vincent Bijlo 2017
English translation © Susan Ridder 2017

First published in Dutch by De Arbeiderpers in 1998
Republished in Dutch by Holland Park Press in 2017

A CIP catalogue record for this book is
available from The British Library.

ISBN 978-1-907320-63-7

Cover designed by Reactive Graphics

Printed and bound by
CPI Group (UK) Ltd, Croydon CR0 4YY

www.hollandparkpress.co.uk

The Institute is a boarding-school novel about a boy who is searching for his identity and a sense of security. It is hilarious and at the same time moving, and paints a frank picture of the 1970s, when 'everything had to be tried out'.

Otto Iking is an outsider, at home as well as at the boarding school for the blind, and he looks at the world around him with an unpitying sense of humour.

He observes the other children as well as the carers and teachers, who aim to prepare their pupils for the able-bodied world, which 'can be very tough'.

He discovers his feelings for Sonia, a fellow student, and he makes plans for a rescue mission to liberate hostages in a notorious Moluccan hijacking case.

But most of all, he wants to escape from the institute for the blind to a school for sighted children. Otto doesn't want sympathy. He can see a future: working for the radio.

In short, a novel about a boy with remarkable powers of observation.

For Mariska, my wife

Thunderstorms. They used to really frighten him.

Not because of the lightning, which he couldn't see, but because of the thunder.

People didn't really understand. They'd say, 'Surely a tough guy like you isn't afraid of a little thunder?'

And he'd say, 'No, but you can see it coming, the thunder, you can see the lightning.'

And then they said, 'Yes, but the lightning frightens us too.'

Which he couldn't understand.

Then there was more thunder. First they were frightened by the lightning, and, when they'd recovered, he was frightened by the thunder. Because the others were so spooked by the lightning, they forgot to tell him there'd be thunder.

Then there was more thunder... And again, and again. It grew louder and louder, but no one warned him. He'd say, 'I think you're not telling me there'll be a bang that'll frighten me on purpose. I think you just want me to get a fright.'

And they'd say, 'You're right. Because you can't warn us of the lightning. If you can't stop us from getting a fright, we don't need to stop you from getting one. That's equality, boy.'

And then there was more thunder. But this time it was so close by that the thunder and lightning came simultaneously, making everyone jump at the same time.

Harry was my example. Harry was the blindest of the blind, a super blind. Harry could do anything, and anything he couldn't do, he'd do at some point.

I could do less than Harry, but I learned from him. He had a head start, because he'd gone blind when he was two, which made a difference, he said. You had already learned more. A tumour had blinded him in both eyes. I had no idea what a tumour was, but Harry could tell very interesting stories about it and reduce even the most horrible people to reverent silence.

Harry had glass eyes, which brought him fame amongst the sighted children. He once came on holiday with us, which proved quite a challenge for my parents. At eight in the morning we'd have children yelling under our bedroom window, demanding that Harry take out his eyes. My Mum got so angry she almost gave him a black eye. Not that she could have, because he had just taken them out, his eyes.

We were resident, which means we lived at the Institute. The Institute was in the town of Bussum, or Huizen, no one really knew. But it didn't matter. If it had been in Laren, it wouldn't have been any better. There were day pupils too, they went home every day. They were the locals, the mother's blind, they didn't belong with us.

We lived in house number 1. Someone had thought it a good idea to name the Institute's lodgings after birds. So house number 1 was called the Blue Tit. Everyone called it the Blind Tit, of course. House number 2 was the Blackbird, number 3 the Finch, and number 4 the Wagtail.

I'd have preferred to stay at one of the other houses, because house number 1 was total madness. Harry and I – my name is Otto, Otto Iking – were the only two normal blind ones there. The rest were smelly, strange, immature, dumb and funny in the head. Looking at the lot of them, you'd think blindness affected the brain. I can remember all their names, their voices, their stupid drivel and their stink, right down to the smallest detail.

First of all there was Walter, of course. He stank of foul soap. Walter's father was a minister, which made his son rather arrogant. He looked down on us a little, although he couldn't see a blind thing more than we could. He made up his own mini sermons, which he delivered to the Blue Tit standing on the cover of the sandpit. His little stories were full of hell and damnation, but they were funny too, particularly because of Walter's high, squeaky voice and rolling Rs. I had never been to church, but I imagined everyone rolling around the floor there, laughing.

Walter always carried a short stick so he wouldn't bump into things. That was ridiculous. No one at the Institute walked around with a stick. Everyone just went wherever, except that stuck-up minister's son. We often took his stick off him, which threw him into a panic, and then he'd bump into everything. That made us roar with laughter. We did it at least four times a week. We couldn't get enough of it. Walter always shouted that that kind of behaviour meant we'd never get to heaven, but that didn't bother us. At Sunday school they'd told us there were no sticks in heaven. It must be boring there, we thought. The place to be was hell, where there were plenty of sticks.

Pieter was a small, whiny boy from Rotterdam. He smelled a little of piss. He used to complain about everyone and everything, saying it was all shite. He was right about that, actually, but there was no point pointing it out all the time. Pieter drove everyone mad, including me. I wasn't the aggressive type, but as soon as Pieter said something, in his high, whiny Rotterdam voice, I felt the muscles in my arms tense and my fists clench. He wore these headgear braces. Once, when he started singing that bloody annoying Feyenoord anthem after a particularly humiliating defeat for Ajax, I knocked those braces right out of his mouth. He had to wear them for another three years as a result.

Michiel was the son of a naval officer. He always wanted to 'kick someone's ass' – that's what they did in the navy, apparently. He never managed to kick anyone though, because he stank of grated Swiss cheese, so you could smell him a mile off. All you needed to do was stick out your leg, and he'd fall. '*That's the way, uh-huh uh-huh, I like it,*' we'd sing. Michiel was very tall and thin. By the time he was twelve, he was bumping his head against the doorposts.

Marc had white hair, we'd been told, so we called him Spitz. Not that we had any idea what a spitz was, but it worked really well – it must be an aggressive breed, we thought. When Marc got angry, we called him 'Tomato with Mayonnaise'. That was Pieter's idea, because Pieter's father was a market gardener and he knew a lot about tomatoes. Marc was musical. He and I used to play beautiful tunes on the recorder.

Tony was deaf and fat and black-skinned, but we didn't know any offensive words for that. Besides, he wouldn't have heard them anyway. Tony got lost everywhere. That boy had such a bad sense of direction that he could lose his way in the toilet. When he didn't know where he was, he'd howl until someone put him back on track. That's how he ended up being called the Foghorn.

Hajo was the tallest, slowest idiot on earth. He was called the Snail. Which was lucky for him because, compared to Hajo, a snail was as fast as a fox. Hajo needed fifteen minutes to walk from school to the Blue Tit, even though it wasn't more than fifty yards. He skipped the milk break.

Eric had epilepsy and was the Fluke, Marga copied everyone and was the Parrot, but her breath was much worse than any bird's could ever be.

As far as Harry and I were concerned, they were all great targets for bullying.

There was only one boy we couldn't beat – Edwin.

Edwin could see a little. No one knew why. Edwin used to kick the completely blind kids in the shins and run

12

away. The staff of the Blue Tit were fine with that because Edwin's head had got stuck during birth. Edwin could do the most awful things and get away with it. He was really underhand, a hypocrite. Everyone really hated him.

Harry and I had set up a bullying competition. We made a list of whom we'd bullied and how often. Tripping up Michiel was five points, beating up Pieter was ten, and so on. We had a table for all the points we could collect. You could lose points too: if you tried to trip up Michiel and failed, five points were taken off your total.

Once I lost nearly all my bullying points when I tried to ring Mr van Halen's doorbell and run away. He worked in the kitchen and lived at the top of the main building, where the Vocational Training School was. I didn't realise that Mr Elmer, the headmaster, was right behind me. Elmer usually smoked a pipe, but not that time, which wasn't very sportsmanlike of him. No sooner had I taken my finger off the bell than he grabbed me by the collar.

'Is that funny?' he bellowed.

'No sir, Mr Elmer, it's not funny,' I squealed. What a spineless wimp I was! It cost me 246 bully points. Now I'd have to trip up Michiel ten times, take Walter's stick off him 38 times, yell 'Spitz' at Marc 46 times, and much, much more in order to bump up my total. And so I did.

Harry could cycle. I could too, but I still crashed into fat Tony regularly. Harry didn't, at least not on purpose. He never fell, never rode into the rhododendrons. I did. Harry had a flat tyre once. Mr Reinier, head of the Blue Tit staff, taught him how to fix it. Just in case he had another flat tyre, which he didn't. I never had a flat tyre either, which was just as well because I didn't know how to fix it and I didn't like Mr Reinier, because if you spelled his name backwards, it was the same.

It happened during our swimming lesson. Mr Mooyman, our swimming, gymnastics and 'how to walk with a stick' instructor, shouted that Tony was *not* to jump off the

13

highest diving board. But Tony was deaf and fat and black-skinned. He jumped right on top of Michiel, paralysing him and putting him in a wheelchair. He moved to another institute, because ours didn't have wheelchair access. We went to see him there once. He still smelled of Swiss cheese, but we couldn't trip him up any more. He was most pitiful and we didn't dare sing *'That's the way, uh-huh uh-huh, I like it'*. After the accident Tony wasn't allowed to jump off the diving board ever again. For that we were truly grateful to Michiel.

We did more than just bully, though, because at times even bullying became a bore at our institute. Everything became a bore, even the weather. As far as I remember, it was always partially cloudy and fifteen degrees. We had Sunday school because there was nothing to do at the weekend. The Institute was a secular institution, but in the battle against boredom sometimes kill-or-cure remedies like Christianity had to be used. Nevertheless, I was the only one who enjoyed Sunday school, which was taught by Reverend van Kampen. He talked very slowly, considered every word before he spoke, rejected it, then said it. And once he'd said something, the next word sounded as if he were sorry the previous one had escaped his mouth. His lessons were far too short. He possessed untold wisdom, that Reverend. He once told us the blind were blind so God's work could manifest itself in them. I used to wait for that all of the rest of Sunday, but nothing manifested itself. I sneezed a couple of times, but that wasn't God's work, it was because the cleaner hadn't done his work properly. Sunday school was much better than our non-Christian weekday school, because that was compulsory.

Weekday school prided itself in individual-oriented teaching. They had no choice really, because it would have been impossible to teach that bunch of imbeciles as a group. There were seven, maybe eight children in our class – which was years four, five and six in one (there weren't that many blind kids) – and our class teacher was Mr Hak.

Braille, that's what they taught me well there. I was already good at it when I was six. Since then, I've embossed tons of paper with dots. I wrote about life outside the gates of the Institute, the life I didn't know. They were always stories about obstinate boys who shouted 'dick' at everyone and trashed their parents' cars and threw up on the table during fancy dinners. Mr Hak read several of my wonderful tales and said that their expensive paper wasn't made for *that*, and that he'd talk to my parents about it. He must have done, because they never ever took me out for a fancy dinner again.

Gerd de Lien's father had bought a new car. It was a Reno. Gerd got in and started the car. Brum brum, bang kaboom went the Reno. He smashed into Uncle Sjoerd's car. Goddamnit, his father shouted, dickhead, and he hit Gerd – smack – on the back. Gerd burst out crying but he hit back and broke his father's glasses and threw up on the table at the Horseshoe that evening, where they had to eat duck with someone to do with the fashion show.

Mr Hak would solemnly say that they had to 'prepare us for the world' at that place. But not for this world, I've since discovered. Step by step our teachers would make us familiar with things from real life, things that might come in useful at some point. We got Play Therapy, for instance. Fifty minutes of it a week with Miss Trudy. Often, when I was playing with the large blocks, she'd go and get a cup of coffee. I'd then quickly build a tower over six foot tall, put it in front of the door and wait under the table. That was the real world, the tower that fell down when Miss Trudy pushed the door, and the coffee that was spilled as a result. But after the tenth time, that too got boring.

Getting us 'ready for the world' with Independence Training. Teaching us to fry eggs and toast cheese sandwiches, tie shoelaces, make tea and eat soup: lemonade soup, that is – a plate full of orange lemonade, which we had to eat with a spoon. Try it blindfolded, it takes hours. The lesson, which we had once a week, lasted only half an hour, so sometimes we spent weeks spooning down a single plateful. At home, my Mum would put soup in mugs, so what happened in the real world was quite different. 'Why make things so difficult then?' I asked, but the answer was that my house wasn't the real world yet.

How could they think that? My house not the real world? My Dad was a press photographer, my Mum designed clothes. We had a Saab and a dog, we knew the mayor of Amstelveen, and that wasn't the real world? People put soup in mugs in the real world, I was sure of that and refused to eat another stupid plate of orange lemonade. Sorry, but it was for my own good, they said. Still, since I was determined, I didn't have to do it. But I'd be sorry. And I was when I went out for a fancy dinner without my parents for the first time – without throwing up on the table, by the way. We were served soup in plates. It was a right mess.

I must have been taught Dutch and arithmetic, but I remember very little of that. Just that we had to recite the multiplication tables. It's the only thing we did as a group and it was very rhythmic. I still know them by heart, those tables.

In the classroom for years four, five and six we had tables from East Germany. They were especially made for the visually impaired, with a top you could angle so that your eyes were closer to the book when you were reading. What nonsense, what a waste of effort. You were better off just learning Braille. But we could flip those lids back with a very loud bang. That's how Mr Hak lost half his index finger, thanks to that stupid Walter. He had absolutely no respect for teachers. Just as well Mr Hak knew how to read Braille with his eyes, so he could do without – the finger, that is.

We had several blind teachers too. Our music teacher was Mr de Wit. Later, he went deaf too. That was a real shame, because he couldn't teach us music any more. We used to shout, 'Hush it, De Wit!' when we passed by his classroom. He had Orff instruments. Perhaps those xylophones and drums contributed to his hearing impairment. We had to sing stupid songs, Dadaist tunes like '*Implantona saxiona ricketicketick America*' and '*un dun dip, in the cup clip, in the cup clip flip, un dun dip*'. No good for anyone's hearing, those children's songs.

Mr de Wit had a dog, Leda. I was afraid of her. I was more frightened of her than of swans, because Leda bit my head. She'd lie stinking and drooling on her doggie stretcher, which I remarked upon in her ear – and then she sank her dirty teeth into my skull. Orff had driven her mad.

In the evenings we had time to ourselves. I used to broadcast radio programmes from the dormitory, which I called Studio Blue Tit. My station was called Radio Fed Up. No one knew why and neither did I. It broadcast the daily Otto Show, which was full of music – mostly George Baker, John Denver, Mud and Jack Jersey, all of which I played on Walter's Grundig Hit Boy tape recorder.

Once in a while I'd interrupt the songs with some light-hearted Institute news. The format for the show was entirely mine, and it was incredibly popular. Everyone tuned in every night. They had to, because as soon as I started broadcasting, you couldn't receive any other programmes.

I'd bought the transmitter from Kenneth, who lived in the same street as my parents. He'd built it from a kit. The Jostikit, it was called. My broadcasts were the best thing the Institute had to offer. And when there was no Institute news, which was quite often, I quoted Bible texts I'd copied from Reverend van Kampen, or read out stories about obstinate boys who threw up on the table. I knew I wanted to work for the radio when I grew up and I figured that broadcasting – albeit illegal – might be the work of

God manifested in me. When I sat down to do my show, the whole world revolved around me, my microphone and my transmitter.

I couldn't get out of bed, of course. It was freezing and the dormitory was unheated. I heard angry footsteps on the stairs, and I knew exactly what was coming.

'It's twelve minutes past eight, and you've got to leave in thirteen minutes,' Miss Letty cried. She snatched the blankets off me. 'Your clothes are on the chair.'

There they were, a T-shirt, jeans, underpants and socks, and, under the chair, a pair of trainers, waiting for the stupidest thing anyone could think of. Shivering as I dressed, I imagined what it would feel like later. Downstairs my cornflakes were waiting, drenched in the milk that Miss Kootje had poured on them fifteen minutes earlier. Miss Kootje didn't like me. It was going to be an awful day. The taxi was two minutes early. Miss Kootje hastily handed me the bag with clothes for later, slapped my bottom, yelped a high-pitched 'best of duck!' (one of her countless supposedly funny puns) and pushed me towards the taxi in the car park. Before I got in, I was kicked in the shins by Edwin. The other children in the taxi were nervous and yelled non-stop, all together, all at once. I said nothing, I was just feeling cold. When I was standing by the side of the pool ten minutes later, it seemed stupider than ever, completely pointless. But I had no more time to think about it, because Mr Mooyman shouted, 'Jump!' and I dropped into the water dressed in my swimming test clothes. I had to swim just one length and I could do it, no doubt about it, but it was so utterly pointless. When I climbed out, I was crying. I cried quite often, I couldn't help it.

'Are you scared?' Mr. Mooyman asked.

'No,' I said, 'I just feel sorry for my clothes, and for Miss Letty, who needs to wash them again.'

He laughed at me and said, 'I thought you were a tough guy.'

I didn't know what that had to do with it. Me, scared? I wasn't scared of anything, except of Mr de Wit's dog Leda, of Edwin and of walking with a stick, which Mr Mooyman knew, because he taught us that too.

Mooyman taught us to find our way independently in the able-bodied world using a stick, which was scary. Not that much could happen. It wasn't all that dangerous to walk around a residential part of Bussum. The worst thing that could happen was getting run over by a child's bike or being disembowelled by a shopping trolley. There was nothing else that could befall you, but I was still scared. Afraid of looking like a fool walking along the pavement waving a crazy stick. I said sorry all the time. When I walked into a lamppost, I said sorry. When I struck my head against a traffic sign, I said sorry. No one has ever apologised to street furniture as often as I did. I apologised to trees when I hit them with my stick, so I was talking to trees long before Dutch Princess Irene. And I said sorry to parked cars when I tapped them by accident. I was really frightened the owners would come tearing out of their houses and beat me up, but they never did. Mr Mooyman himself was angry with me once when I hit *his* car, but I didn't say sorry then. I wasn't sorry at all.

Because Mr Mooyman was ridiculously proud of his car, a middle-class Opel Kadett, or a crap Kadett, my Dad would call it. We had a Saab, after all. Mr Mooyman had covers made of some kind of artificial fur for the front seats, so they'd wear out less quickly and it'd keep its trade-in value. But the covers were so thick the doors couldn't close properly, you really had to slam them. When he went to trade in the car, the Kadett garage told him it was a total write-off because the doors had been damaged due to those fur covers. I never heard my Dad laugh so loudly when I told him that.

After fifty lessons of walking with a stick I had to take a test. Since I'd passed my swimming test the day before, I wasn't really scared any more. I only said sorry when I stepped into a dog turd. The test was an hour's walk through the centre of Bussum, its bustling town centre full of clothes racks on the pavements, flower stalls, strategically

20

placed bollards, casually parked cars and random bin bags. In other words, everything that can turn a stick test into an unforgettably cheerful and exciting hour. I wore the same clothes I'd worn for the swimming test. After all, they'd already been through quite a lot. Even if I poked a hole in the aquarium at the pet shop, I'd be fine. I was a hero that day and couldn't possibly fail my exam. It didn't bother me in the slightest that the roads were icy. My clothes could cope with water, frozen or otherwise.

Too bad for Mr Mooyman *he* wasn't wearing his swimming test clothes. After forty yards, I heard him fall, swearing. I didn't say sorry, I carried on – convinced there was a world record to be achieved. I was the first blind person who, in the most terrible circumstances ever, would clock a time that even super blind Harry could only dream of. I heard other people fall – thud, thud, thud – the street was full of groaning and swearing, but I carried on. I knew the route like the back of my hand. Then I heard puffing and grating noises behind me, as well as the ominous hum of an engine approaching at speed. At first I thought it was Mooyman in his crap Kadett, but it couldn't be this noisy, could it? When the noise was right beside me, it was so loud that I couldn't hear the clicking of my stick against the pavement any more.

Then I felt the pavement slip from under my feet.

'Smart aleck!'

It came from afar, but I quickly realised who'd said it. It was Mr Mooyman, and the way he said it was unmistakable. It sounded like he was smiling, though. He liked blind people who take the initiative. A woman's voice close to my ear said that I should try and sit up. I didn't even know I was lying down, but I managed. I felt sheets and blankets – this was a bed.

'The Majella,' said Mooyman. 'You're in the Majella.'

The Majella. It sounded frightening, which it had been three years before, when I'd been admitted for my tonsils. Mooyman explained what had happened.

'You were doing great,' he said, 'then a gritter messed things up.'

'What's the matter with me?' I asked.

'A gash in your head. It was full of grit, your head, when you were brought in.'

I didn't dare touch my head, I was worried that I might be able to feel and damage my brain, making me as stupid as the other blind kids. I felt strange, dizzy, but wasn't in any pain. Perhaps there was grit in my brain. I tried to think – successfully. I thought of Harry and how he'd laugh when he heard about my accident.

I didn't have to stay in the Majella and was discharged that very same day. I had twelve stitches. Miss Letty came to pick me up in a taxi.

Uncle Jan, the driver, was cheerful. 'Hey, look at you. You look like a pirate. Had problems with the radar?'

Miss Letty laughed out loud and stroked my head, a little too roughly.

When I got to the Blue Tit, it was chaos. Harry had lost his eyes. He'd taken out his eyes to impress the new intern and put them on the table. Then he'd been called to the phone. It was his father. You don't need eyes to talk on the phone but when he wanted to put them back afterwards, they were gone. They suspected the intern. Her handbag was searched and many things were found, including eye

22

shadow, but no eyes. She realised she'd failed. On her very first day at the Blue Tit at that. While Harry was on the phone, she should have kept an eye on his eyes.

At that point Eric had an epileptic fit and all eyes turned to him, except Harry's. I went to the dormitory, because it was time for Radio Fed Up's daily broadcast. There was no music that evening. I just gave a detailed account of the slippery stick test, my heroic stay at the Majella and my twelve stitches. I also called for the murder of that underhand, hypocritical, visually impaired boy, Edwin. This was a daily item that'd had no effect, unfortunately. I also took the opportunity to say that Harry's eyes had disappeared. The extra police message I slipped in asked everyone to look out for a pair of shiny blue eyes. When I ended the show with the national anthem, as I did every day, Harry came upstairs. He hadn't been listening. Before going to sleep, I told him about the Majella. I let him touch the plaster on the gash in my head. He didn't laugh at me.

'Cool, man, twelve stitches,' he said.

He was very impressed. I fell asleep contented.

Mr van Halen distributed the food from the central kitchen in large steel tins that always smelled the same, no matter what food was in them. Miss Kootje used to call them 'bins', of course. Hilarious.

We used to get a hot meal at lunchtime, hot and disgusting. Purslane and endive. Peas and carrots, good for your eyes. Streaky bacon-wrapped mince rolls and sausages, plenty of reasons to become a vegetarian. And always, always, those over-boiled potatoes. Van Halen brought our soup-kitchen food in an aluminium food cart with air-filled tyres. There was a door on its side, through which he passed the tins.

The following day, Harry, still eyeless, said, 'I bet you don't dare getting into that cart.'

Well, he was wrong. I climbed in and sat down in a puddle of gravy. The space was so small that I needed to curl up. Harry banged the door shut and pushed the cart past the Blue Tit, the Blackbird, the Finch and the Wagtail. We sped along like a rocket, because the road sloped steeply down to the sports ground.

'You've got my eyes!' Harry yelled.

Where the hell did he get that idea? Me, his best friend!

'I haven't!' I shouted in reply.

The sound of my voice took me by surprise, it was deafeningly loud in that smelly, confined metal box.

'You have!' Harry yelled. Then he let go of the cart and ran away. The cart began to rock and, rolling on at great speed, veered off the road, carried on for some distance on just two wheels, then flipped over. It bumped into a tree and fell on its side, on the side with the door. I was trapped.

'I'll go and look for your eyes!' I shouted.

No answer. I was going to die in that ever tighter, almost airtight, container, I was sure of that. I'd be served up by Van Halen the next day, wolfed down unenthusiastically, like the rest of the food. I tried to topple the cart by pushing hard against the bottom with my back, but it didn't move. By the time I heard my rescue in the distance, I could barely breathe.

'Keep going. Come on, those trees are hardly going to move onto the path, you know!'

It was Mr Mooyman walking a group of blind children towards the sports ground. I began to bang and shout – as much as I still could. Mooyman pulled the cart upright, only for it to fall over again, as one of the wheels had fallen off. He tried again, turned it 180 degrees, put it on its other side and pulled open the door, which was now above me.

'What *are* you doing? Do you want a season ticket for the Majella?'

I sucked in the fresh air and clambered out of the wreckage of the food cart. I was dripping with gravy, there was a tuft of purslane on my head, and the gash in my head from walking with a stick had opened up. When I was able to stand on both legs again, half a mince roll dropped out of one of the legs of my trousers. The cart was as much of a write-off as Mooyman's crap Kadett, and I had to go and explain it to Mr Elmer. But not before I'd stopped at the clinic. We had a real clinic, as quite a few people ended up with injuries at the Institute. My head wound was treated by Nurse Pauka.

Elmer puffed on his pipe and blew a cloud of smoke into my face. I kept my jaws firmly shut.

'How can a cart with you inside' – his voice sounded more threatening than when I'd rung the bell and run away – 'again, how can a cart with you *inside* crash on the sports ground?'

Although I thought Harry was a real jerk at that point, I wasn't going to betray him.

'Am I speaking Spanish?' Elmer bellowed.

No, he wasn't.

'Edwin,' I mumbled.

'I've heard enough! You can go – and you don't need to go to school this afternoon.'

At the Blue Tit everyone began to fuss over me, and for once I was okay with that. I had a shower and was allowed to put on clean clothes. This was unusual, because usually we were allowed just one change a week. And when I went downstairs, I was given coffee with hot milk, a treat we were normally only given on feast days. After that, I lay in my bed for a while.

The police came. Edwin was summoned from the classroom and all Blue Tit residents sat down at the round table with the greasy plastic tablecloth. I asked one of the officers, the one sitting next to me, whether he had a gun.

'Sure,' he said, and he gave it to me. I aimed at the spot where Edwin was sitting and pulled the trigger. Edwin and his chair fell over backwards, and then I was woken up by Harry bursting into the dormitory.

'You have to give them back!' he screamed.

'I don't have them,' I said, 'but I know where they could be. Edwin's got them.'

At that point, Edwin kicked Harry in the shins, ran away and tripped over the doorstep. I've never felt as good about anyone's misfortune as I did then. It sounded like he was in a lot of pain, and all three members of staff came rushing in to take care of him – oh oh oh. No one looked at the bruise on Harry's leg. No one believed there was one. Edwin would never do such a thing.

After dinner that evening I talked to Harry in private. We sat in the log cabin on the lawn behind the Blue Tit. It was quite a childish construction, four walls made of thin tree trunks with a plank on top and a hole on the side. It had been donated by an organisation that wanted to do something for the blind. A waste of all those trees that had been sacrificed for it. If only the organisation had asked us what we wanted. But no, they knew exactly what was good for us. We'd once tried to set the log cabin on fire, but had been caught red-handed by Edwin, who'd reported us to the staff, of course. We were forbidden to enter the cabin, and that's why we were there. That's what made it attractive again.

'So Edwin's got them?' said Harry. 'How do you

know?'

'That's what he said.'

'I don't believe you.'

'Really. You know how he's always talking to himself? Well, I was in the toilet this afternoon and heard him, he was inside another cubicle, saying that he'd put them in the petrol tank of Mr Reinier's moped.'

Mr Reinier had a moped. But he was off duty that night, so Harry couldn't ask him if he'd by any chance found a pair of eyes in his petrol tank. He had to wait until the next morning. That night I sent another police message out into the ether, but I didn't breathe a word about the accident with the cart. No one else needed to know.

The next day Mr Reinier told us his moped had been stolen the night before. I promised that my next broadcast would also include a police message for him.

The police came. We all sat down at the dining table with the greasy plastic tablecloth, all of us except Edwin. He was nowhere to be found. I asked one of the officers, the one sitting next to me, whether he had a gun. I thought they'd come to confiscate the Jostikit. Broadcasting was illegal, after all, so I thought it a good idea to first check if the officers were armed.

'No,' he said, 'we're plain-clothes policemen.'

I didn't know what that meant, but thought it better not to ask.

'Well then,' the other plain-clothes policeman said. 'So your eyes have been stolen.'

Good, it was about the eyes.

'Yes, officer,' Harry replied. 'They were in Mr Reinier's tank.'

'His *tank*? Is he doing his alternative National Service here in a tank?'

'No, he's got a moped.'

'And the eyes have been stolen from the moped's petrol tank?'

'No, the moped has been stolen, with the eyes in the tank.'

'How did those eyes get in the tank?'

'Edwin did it.'

'How do you know?'

'That's what Otto says.'

'And who's Otto?'

'That's me,' I said. 'Edwin's head was stuck during birth, that's why he talks to himself, and I heard him say that he was planning to put the eyes in the tank.'

'Thanks, Otto. So where's Edwin?'

Nobody knew and the officers didn't feel like looking for him. They wrote a report about the offence, because that was why they had come. Harry needed a police report saying his eyes were stolen for the insurance company, otherwise the insurers wouldn't pay up. Two days later, the plain-clothes policemen returned. As a result of a tip-

28

off – no doubt from someone who had listened to Radio Fed Up – they'd arrested a minor who was in possession of Mr Reinier's moped. They'd checked the tank at the police station, but found nothing. The minor had been sent on his way. Now he was free, probably with Harry's eyes in his pocket.

I was fascinated by the moped. As soon as I knew for certain Mr Reinier wasn't looking, I'd check it out and experiment with it until I could get it started.

I discovered I could do it. There was a lever on the side of the moped, just above the pedals. If you pulled it and then stepped on a pedal, the engine started. The right-hand handle was for accelerating. Half an hour later I pulled it off its stand.

I drove it.

I moved slowly, but I drove. The sound of the motor echoing off the buildings told me where I was. I headed down the road, past the car park, the reception, the kitchen, the main building, the clinic, the laundry room, the printing office and the primary school, then back to the Blue Tit. I switched off the motor and flipped out the stand. It was parked exactly as it had been before. Mr Reinier would never know.

I decided I'd get a moped when I was older. Driving a moped was so much more fun than cycling.

Meanwhile the food had arrived. I could smell it from afar. It was chips, but that wasn't necessarily something to get too excited about, because they'd have been in Van Halen's cart for twenty minutes, getting soggy. Still, some of the children were always happy when there were chips. Which said a lot about them. They were really stupid, they hadn't learned a thing from their previous experiences with chips. But things were different this time, the chips were crisp, hot – and nicely browned, Edwin said. Jerk. He always had to remind us that he could see. The food wasn't from the kitchen today, Miss Letty explained proudly. She'd fried the chips herself, because Van Halen's cart was

29

broken. Everyone cheered. Thanks to my accident, at least we got good chips.

After lunch we had an extra-long lesson. No one knew why it was called a 'block lesson', but it meant that it wasn't taught by Hak. This time it was Mr van Staveren, the physics teacher. We were going to learn how to siphon, using two buckets of water – one on a table and another on a chair. We had to take a tube, put one end in the bucket on the table, suck at the other end until we got water in our mouths, then put that end into the other bucket on the chair. And lo! The water from the table bucket flowed into the chair bucket. Fantastic. The principle of siphoning begged to be tried out. After school Harry and I would try a second time to set fire to the log cabin. What Van Staveren had taught us that afternoon would come in handy, and make him an accomplice. I went to the moped, unscrewed the cap, put the tube into the tank and sucked at the other end until I got the petrol in my mouth. The taste of petrol is incomparable. Greasy, spicy, salty and acid all at the same time. I accidentally swallowed a little. It felt like I was on fire. If I'd struck a match, I'd have exploded. Soon, the petrol stopped flowing into our bucket. We only had a little, not enough to set fire to the log cabin.

But we couldn't do it just then anyway, because Piss Pieter was playing cowboys and Indians in there, all by himself.

'He's an Ajax fan, that dumb-ass Winnetou,' he cried. 'Oohoohoohoohoo.'

You could hear his braces twang. The idiot didn't even have an Indian headdress. I had one, and a cowboy suit, and a real holster, but they were at my parents'.

So Harry and I did some bouncing first. Bouncing was seesawing the rough way. The seesaw was next to the log cabin, and it was the only nice plaything on the lawn behind the Blue Tit. It was high too, so you could fly up to a yard above your seat when you kicked hard. The bucket toppled when we bounced and the petrol dripped out, soaked into the ground. Then we heard Mr Reinier drive off, so we knew we couldn't get any more. Oh well, the cabin could wait. At least we now knew how to siphon.

In the evening, my parents came to visit. They had been to a cremation in the area. My Mum said I stank of petrol. She stank too, of some disgusting perfume. They acted very formally and I didn't know what to say. So I showed them how to siphon – with water. They were very impressed.

Their visits never made me happy, they didn't belong there. Parents were supposed to stay at home, be visited once a month. That was hard enough. I didn't know them very well. I doubted I was actually their child. When I asked, they became angry. Perhaps I'd have understood them better if they had had normal jobs, if my Dad had been a carpenter and my Mum a cashier. The other children's parents all had fairly straightforward professions, like farmer, market gardener or officer in the navy. But what do you make of a press photographer and a clothes designer? None of the blind kids knew that clothes were designed. As far as they were concerned, clothes were just pieces of cloth that hung on your body. As for pictures, it didn't matter what they depicted because when you touched them, they all felt the same. But you weren't supposed to do that, it left grease stains. As if that made any difference to us. Oh, the formality of such visits! The way they asked Miss Kootje how things were with 'our Otto'. Things weren't too good for our Otto at that particular moment, but our Otto didn't tell them, because our Otto wasn't asked any questions. All parents walked around the Institute as if visiting the isolation ward of a lunatic asylum for the very first time, a closed ward where a distant cousin was being treated. My parents were no exception. Parents needed to stay at home, while we stayed there.

So I told my parents about the next day. It was going to be a big day. Surinam had become independent two years previously and President Ferrier was visiting the

Netherlands. He planned to visit the Institute because he wanted to establish something similar in Surinam. I could give him lots of useful tips. For instance: don't get a log cabin and do get tasty food – but that wasn't a problem in Surinam. Apparently they ate rotis every day, which were delicious. We had them once during 'Surinam week'. Ferrier wasn't coming on his own, he was to be accompanied by Princess Margriet and her husband, Pieter van Vollenhoven. We, years four, five and six, were to have the honour of doing gymnastics for the President and their Royal Highnesses. My parents didn't show much interest. They started talking about the cremation again. As far as I was concerned, they might as well have dropped dead right then. I'd have quite happily doused them in petrol siphoned from Mr Reinier's moped.

Finally, they left. They wanted to be home before dark. Nonsense. They just wanted to get away from me. Going home in the dark wasn't a problem at all. We could *cycle* in the dark, couldn't we? And we didn't even have lights on our bikes.

'Kon hesi baka', we were to shout the next day, when Mr Ferrier was leaving the Institute. We practised one more time before going to sleep. After that, there was an extra Otto show about the following day, featuring Surinam expert Fat Tony, expert because he was black. But he was deaf too, so he couldn't hear my questions. At the end of the conversation I discovered he wasn't from Surinam, he was from Curaçao. That night I dreamt of shouting *'kon hesi baka'* at my Mum. 'Come back soon,' it meant. I didn't mean a word of it.

At ten to nine the following morning we sat in the classroom dressed in our Sunday best. We were the model class. This is where the visit was to begin. After visiting us, our illustrious guests were to be given a tour by Mr Elmer, while we dashed down to the gym, changed, and waited to do our performance. Following the gymnastics display, a group of six carefully selected blind kids was to guide the party, without any help from sighted people, to the car park, after which the visit would be over.

We could hear the visitors approach from afar. A helicopter circled above the Institute. Everyone in the class got very excited. Then the door opened. Luckily the hinges were squeaky, so I could hear what was happening. There they were. Mr Hak suddenly became very formal.

'These are my pupils,' he said. 'Our system is entirely geared to the individual needs of our pupils. Harry, could you please tell us what you're doing at the moment?'

Harry didn't have pupils, because he still hadn't found his eyes. He'd been given a pair of glasses for the day, to avoid embarrassment.

'I'm doing sums with an abacus,' Harry said. 'The abacus is a Chinese frame with five beads on every wire, four under the bar, and one above it. The bead above the bar is worth five beads, so on a single wire you can count to nine. This one was made by Mr Splinter.'

'Yes,' Mr Hak said. 'Mr Splinter teaches at the Technical School, which you'll be shown later. That's where these abacuses are made. As you can see, we are self-sufficient. Otto, could you tell us what kind of instrument you have in front of you?'

'It's a *piegt*,' I said, 'a tool with which to write Braille. The *piegt* was invented by Mr Piegt. Peter Piegt is the name of the inventor. The *piegt* is used for writing Braille, which was invented by Mr Braille. And the paper we write on was invented by Mr Tsai Lun from China, in about 105 AD. Now I'll type some Braille for you.'

I wrote: shit shit dick dick shit dick dick shit.

'I wrote that I'm very happy you're here.'

They mumbled something, deeply touched. Then Mr Hak asked some questions of the others, who were using different types of Braille game boards. Margriet, Pieter and President Ferrier now know what they look like. Then they went out with Mr Elmer for the tour and we rushed down to the gym.

33

The gym was small and entirely made of wood. There was a rubber strip on the floor near the walls. This was the walking track, which we used for marching and jogging, accompanied by Mr Mooyman on piano. We did our gymnastics bare-bodied and barefoot. We didn't see the point of being bare-bodied, but being barefoot meant we could feel the track.

The plan was for us to first do some marching and jogging, then to 'jump the cord' and finally, to do some exercises on the apparatuses. Since Mr van Vollenhoven – an accomplished pianist – was present, Mooyman was going to play drums that day, rather than the piano. The marching and jogging went well, without anyone bumping into anyone else and without any pestering. On any other occasion, we'd have pinched each other whenever we could. Even Edwin didn't kick anyone.

For 'jumping the cord' a piece of elastic cord was stretched over the width of the room, right in the middle, about two feet off the floor. We stood at one end and behind us were our guests, seated on an improvised stand. Mooyman called out our names. When you'd heard your name, you had to jog to the other side of the room and jump over the cord. I had to go first. I jumped too early. There was laughter behind me. I jumped again and they laughed again, louder this time. I'd jumped too early again. Then I made a third attempt, followed by a roar of laughter and applause. I'd done it. I turned around and waved. Great – success at last. I completed the rest of the exercises in a blur, floating above the asymmetric bars, vaulting with ease and climbing the rope like a monkey. Afterwards, I was allowed to shake hands with the entire delegation.

'Hello Otto, I'm Princess Margriet,' the princess said.

'My parents live near your park,' I said.

'I beg your pardon?'

'The Princess Margriet Park.'

It was wonderful. As I changed my clothes, I felt like the Ajax captain who'd just received the World Champions'

Cup. Mooyman slapped me on the back and put me first in the line of pupils selected to accompany the party to the car park. I was given a push, meaning it was time to go. Outside, the helicopter still hovered in the air. I'd never heard anything so loud, it was louder than the gritter. Silly of Mooyman not to have thought of that, we were completely disoriented and some security staff had to step in to put us back on track. I heard Mooyman call out, but I couldn't hear what he said. '*Kon hesi baka*,' I kept shouting, but my voice was lost in the roar of the blades, and then they were gone.

We had rotis for dinner, but they didn't taste good because they'd been made in the soup kitchen. They tasted of purslane. I guessed Van Halen had got a new cart.

On the Radio Fed Up *kon hesi baka* special that night, I talked about the successful visit of the president of the young nation to the former motherland. Afterwards the dormitory reeked of endive roti farts. *Kon hesi baka*, I whispered into my pillow, knowing that that afternoon had been the highlight of my time at the Institute, on that track in the gym, with that cord. It made me sad.

At three o'clock there was a thunderstorm and even though thunderstorms really scared me, I hoped that the lightning would strike and burn the entire Institute, with me in it, to the ground. But that didn't happen. The next morning there were soggy cornflakes as usual.

I had to retake my stick test that day, without swimming-test clothes this time. My Mum had objected to them during her visit two nights previously and had thrown them out. They were too shabby, she thought. I'd have to do it entirely without armour this time.

I was far from heroic. The only thing worth mentioning is that I knocked over a wooden sign shaped like a cone of fries outside a snack bar. I passed. From then on I was allowed to go wherever I wanted with a stick.

I could, for instance, go to the petrol station on Huizerweg. They sold Coke and crisps and cigarettes. I was planning to smoke, even though I was just eleven. The only thing I needed to find out was the name of the cigarettes. I knew that Drum was rolling tobacco because I remembered an advertisement on Radio North Sea: '*Roll, roll a Drum for each other.*' But I couldn't see myself rolling anything for anyone. Who'd teach me? No, I'd buy ready-made ciggies. But which ones? After the test I asked Mooyman which brand he smoked.

'Camels,' he said, and lit one. It smelled good; that was the brand for me too. I wanted to buy them that very day, because the day after we were going camping in Dwingeloo. I wasn't looking forward to it, but at least I'd have something to smoke there. The camp wasn't compulsory, and Harry wasn't going. I was all on my own. My parents could have taken me home, but they had said it wasn't convenient just then. I couldn't concentrate on anything the rest of the day. After the test I had a one-to-one lesson with Mr Hak, breaking my back doing long division on the abacus. Then an extra-long hour with Mr van Staveren. After the lesson about siphoning he talked about communicating vessels. Not very interesting, I couldn't think of any practical use for it.

My own stick was much heavier than the one I'd been given by Mr Mooyman. That'd been a single piece of fibre glass, and mine was made up of five pieces. You could fold it up but, thanks to the steel cable that ran through it, it was very heavy. After just a hundred yards my hand already hurt. I hadn't even made it out of the grounds yet. I thought about turning back, but quickly dismissed the idea. I was on an important mission. I had to walk past the reception, through the gate, turn right, walk along the service road, cross the service road at the motorway flyover, cross the flyover and then turn left. That's where the petrol pump was. Cyclists are impossible to hear, so it wasn't my fault that I pushed my stick into the spokes of a bicycle when crossing the service road. The cyclist fell and said sorry. I didn't. I was glad I had my own stick, the fibre-glass one

36

would almost certainly have broken.

Since I couldn't tell if there was a queue when I entered the shop at the petrol station, I stayed by the door. I thought that at some point I'd be asked how they could help me, but that didn't happen.

'Are you with someone?' a woman asked.

I didn't know what to say, I didn't know the answer.

'Is it my turn yet?' I asked.

'It's my turn, pump number three,' she said loudly to the man behind the counter.

Then it was my turn.

'Which pump?' the man behind the counter asked.

'No pump. A packet of paprika crisps, a can of Coke and a packet of Camels, please.'

'A packet of what?'

'Camels.'

'Ah, the cigarettes. You're a connoisseur, sir. With or without?'

What the hell did he mean by that?

'With,' I said. Fries without mayo weren't nice either. So that was what my stick test had yielded: crisps, Coke and Camels, purchased for seven guilders without the help of anyone sighted. I was proud, incredibly proud of the fact I'd achieved all that. I walked back twice as fast as I had on the way there.

'I need to speak to you for a minute, Otto,' Miss Letty said when I came in through the back door carrying my bag of groceries. 'What are those cigarettes for?'

How could she know I bought cigarettes?

'I don't have any cigarettes.'

'What's in the bag, then?'

'Coke and crisps.'

'And cigarettes. I don't mean to be rude, but my eyes are fine and the bag is transparent.'

'They're not for me, they're for Mr Mooyman, because I passed my stick test.'

She laughed and took my hand.

'Come,' she said, 'we'll take them to him.'

Mooyman had the afternoon off on Wednesdays but was still around, drinking coffee in the staff room.

'Otto's got something for you, Pim,' Miss Letty said.

'Yes,' I said. 'Because my test went so well this morning, I bought you a packet of Camels.'

'Boy oh boy, thank you very much, Otto. When I'm in the Majella with lung cancer, I'll think of you.'

We walked back to the Blue Tit, where it was eerily quiet inside.

'Let's go upstairs for a minute,' Miss Letty said.

We went to the waiting room, the staff bedroom, a small room with a bed and a nightstand. We sat down on the bed, and after a long silence, she said, 'We found Harry's eyes in your nightstand.'

Jesus.

'Who looked in my nightstand?'

'It was open. And there's a crack in the left eye. How did those eyes end up in your nightstand?'

'Do you remember the night when Harry took out his eyes to impress the new intern, and how he couldn't find them when he wanted to put them back in?'

'Yes.'

'And do you remember where we were then?'

'Who do you mean by "we"?'

'You and me.'

'You and me? I have no idea.'

'You came to pick me up from the Majella that evening. You came by taxi.'

'Yes,' she said. 'With Uncle Jan.'

'Exactly,' I said. 'So who could never have had those eyes?'

'Otto Iking.'

'And who else?'

'Miss Letty. You sound like Sherlock Holmes.'

'So we both have an alibi.'

'Okay,' she said, 'but then how did those eyes end up in

38

your nightstand?'

'Edwin,' I said. 'He left the door open on purpose, so everyone would suspect me.'

We went looking for him, but he was nowhere to be found, of course. However, I knew that, like me, he was meant to go camping. I could kill him at the campsite. But first I'd torture him. I'd cut out his dirty eyes, then bash his stupid head against the ground until the few brains he had were pulp. Then I'd cut open his stomach, tear out his intestines and use them to strangle him. Harry had left already, picked up by his parents. No doubt he thought I'd actually stolen his eyes. He probably hated me. I couldn't find my Coke and crisps anywhere either. Everything sucked. I went and sat on the horse outside, which wasn't meant for eleven-year-old men, but I couldn't think of anything better to do.

Miss Letty was sweet. She said she'd talk to the rest of the staff and tell them my story. She was convinced by it. But the rest of the staff would never take any action against Edwin, because his head had got stuck during birth, so he couldn't help himself. I had no sympathy for him whatsoever. He had signed his own death warrant. That's what I was thinking as I was rocking on the horse, which was attached to a spring. Suddenly, startling me, there was panting behind me. It was Edwin. He was always panting, because he did nothing but run around all day. I wanted to get off, but it was too late. He grabbed the horse's tail, pulled the horse backwards, then let go. The horse sprang forward and launched me like a rocket. I landed on the grass. Now I was absolutely certain: he had to die. As soon as possible. That boy was so sneaky, such a hypocrite. I liked bullying, but one needed to be open and honest about it. I'd kill him in Dwingeloo. I owed it to both Harry and myself. When walking back for evening sandwiches at the Blue Tit, I solemnly vowed I'd do it.

We played a silly, childish game during the meal. Edwin behaved as if nothing had happened. Miss Kootje began.

'I'm going camping in Dwingeloo and I'll take a plate. Now it's your turn, Otto.'

'I'm going camping in Dwingeloo and I'll take a plate and a gun.'

'Oh come on, just play the game. Why would you take a gun?' Miss Kootje said.

'Well, it could come in handy.'

'Okay then, as you wish, a gun.'

We carried on like this for another half-hour, eating raisin rolls that tasted like cardboard and Kingcorn bread. Which was worse than T bread. I'd also take to Dwingeloo: a knife, a piece of rope and a flail. That's a spiked lead ball on a chain, used in the Middle Ages and very good to wave around. When we did the dishes, five plates were broken. Something was broken every day, but this was unusual, because it was Miss Letty who did it. Walter laughed out loud, almost sadistically, and she started to cry. I nearly cried myself. I wanted to console her, but I didn't dare.

After the dishes it was my turn to have a bath. You got to have a bath once a week. It used to be more often, but once we made such a mess that several important documents in the office below were damaged. From then on we had to take a shower instead. The showers were in the other bathroom, but every Wednesday someone was allowed to take a bath on their own, without splashing.

I discovered something about my willy in the bath. Or rather, my duck discovered it. Rocking on the tiny waves I made, it bumped against my willy, which grew as a result. I felt something too, as if I needed to pee, but much more pleasant. I thought, SUPERCALIFRAGILISTICEXPIALIDOCIOUS! That's what Mary Poppins used to say. That's what this was, SUPERCALIFRAGILISTICEXPIALIDOCIOUS. Someone downstairs called up that I needed to come out of the bath and pack for tomorrow. There was no time for a Radio Fed Up broadcast. My large audience would have to do without me for a while, because I couldn't take the transmitter to

40

Dwingeloo. That would be too dangerous.

I thought of my duck that night, and my willy grew again.

'We're going to Dwingeloo, we're going to Dwingeloo!' everyone sang the next morning, in the Volkswagen van Mr Reinier was driving. Mrs Reinier was there too, she sang the loudest of all. I didn't, I was thinking of my duck. I hadn't got it with me because there was no bath in Dwingeloo. We were going camping, which I'd never done before. My Dad had once spent a night in a tent in Schoorl when he was young, which had been terrible because the tent had been blown away. That's why we always rented a holiday home. It was always windy there too, by the way, but the house never got blown away.

Spirits were high in that van. Camping must be fantastic, I thought. What had I been missing out on all those years? Or was it the rain getting everyone's spirits up? I didn't expect much of camping. It sounded scary, it had the word 'camp' in it. When my Mum talked about the war, she always talked about 'the camps', and things had been awful there.

We had to stop for petrol on the way and I asked if I could sit in the front seat, so I could change gears. That way at least I could contribute to the high spirits. I could change gears really well. But Mrs Reinier wasn't interested.

'No,' she said, 'I'll stay with my brave knight.'

Mr Reinier a brave knight? What sort of woman was she?

'Hey Otto, you grumpy socks, why don't you join in?' Miss Kootje said.

'We're going to Dwingeloo,' I sang, but at that very moment we arrived and it stopped raining. It started pouring instead.

It was so wet that we couldn't pitch our tents. So we sat listlessly in the campsite canteen. There was a table football set there, a table with bars that had figurines attached to them. You could turn the bars and move the players backwards and forwards. There was a small ball on the table that you had to try and hit with your players. Hajo's bars hit me in the stomach and no one knew who

42

was winning. It was really boring. No one was in a good mood any more and finally I began to feel at ease again. Everyone was back to normal.

Until the sun came out.

Then they started singing again.

It was dry outside, so we needed to pitch the tents. They wanted to teach me how to put up a tent, but rain threatened, so it had to be done quickly.

When it began to rain again, I was allowed to go back inside. Which was just as well, as I didn't expect to ever need to put up a tent again. Then the rain stopped and it was dry enough, even, for the cooking to be done outside. We all had to sit still, though, because there were burners. And the goo that was dolloped onto my plate was so disgusting that I began to long for Mr van Halen's cart.

Kitchen duty. I quickly discovered this meant washing up with a sponge, no brush, in a tub filled with cold water. Otto was the fall guy and he scrubbed the plates so well that all plasters with the names of the owners in Braille were scrubbed off. It didn't matter, the food wouldn't be any better for it. Nor worse, that would have been impossible. The tea towel was fastened with a clothes peg to a guy rope, a nasty rope that was to keep your tent up and that I tripped over at least thirty times. I had thought that all tents were like the wigwam at my parents' place, the one in which I played cowboys and Indians in my cowboy suit with my Indian headdress on and a real holster on my hips. But this tent was different, hence the guy ropes. Why didn't anyone ever tell me anything? I had to find out for myself what things looked like. This tent was ridiculous, you could hardly sit up in it, that's how low it was. I had to share it with Hajo the Snail, who announced he was going to 'take up quarters'. This turned out to mean nothing more than putting a sleeping bag on a sleeping mat. I decided to take up quarters myself, even though I didn't have a mat. How was I supposed to know you need a sleeping mat when you go camping? No one ever told me.

43

After my kitchen duty there was the evening programme. We could choose between playing football and cycling on a tandem. Before I could make my choice, all the tandems were gone: taking up quarters had taken me a whole quarter of an hour. After all I was just a layman as far as camping was concerned, with a cheap sleeping bag whose limitations I was to discover a few hours later.

Football was fun. We played with a heavy rubber ball with bells, so you could hear it coming. You had to play it close to the ground, otherwise you couldn't hear the bells. Anyway, it was hard to kick it high up, because it weighed six and a half pounds. Sometimes, when the ball lay still, it could take minutes for anyone to find it. You had to play with your arms stretched out in front of you, in case you bumped into someone else. The Volkswagen minibus served as a goal. Edwin had to defend it, because he could see a little, which is handy if you're the goalkeeper. He kicked the ball far above the field – straight into my stomach. The staff didn't see a thing, they were blinder to some things than we were. He should have been shown a red card and banned from playing sports for the rest of his life. Just you wait, boy, I thought. Tomorrow we're going for a walk on the mud flats, after which you'll never be able to play any sport ever again.

But first I had to get through the night – in my cheap sleeping bag. Five minutes after I'd taken off my clothes, I had to put them back on again. I lay on my back and thought of the duck waiting for me at home.

'Do you have something that excites you?' I asked Hajo the Snail.

'No,' he said in his stupid snail voice, 'but my father does.'

'Does it make his willy grow?'

'I don't know. Well, maybe, because the other day he said he wants to buy a bigger car.'

He fell asleep, the only thing he could do quickly. I stayed awake, he snored. I never knew that the ground could be so hard. But I must have fallen asleep at some point, because I woke feeling the urgent need to take a crap. Opening several zips, I quickly worked my way out and set off. The loo, I guessed, was probably in the building where we had to brush our teeth. No one had told me about it, but to my surprise and great relief, I found the building. I discovered it had sinks and showers, but no loos. Where were they? I panicked. If you really need to crap, your brain and sense of direction freeze up. I wandered desperately around the field. Burners were knocked over, I tripped over guy ropes and stepped on a plastic plate, which broke. Eventually I squatted and did my number two, the best ever. I wiped my bum with a piece of paper I found lying in the grass nearby. In order to find my way back, I wandered across the field until I bumped into a tent and felt around for a guy rope with a tea towel hanging on it. After the fourth rope, I finally felt a tea towel, but it wasn't mine, because mine was slightly torn. I kicked the heavy rubber ball, which rolled against the Volkswagen. One nil. I knew the van was close to our tent. Ah yes, there was the tea towel with the tear. Two nil. Satisfied, I stretched out in my cheap sleeping bag.

At nine o'clock the next morning we were in the van and on our way to the village of Pieterburen on the North coast, heading for a walk on the mud flats. But Mr Reinier couldn't find the visitor centre.

'I don't have the address,' he said. 'Someone crapped on the directions last night.'

'Yes,' Mrs Reinier said, 'what a disgusting turd. I put my foot in it, it was right outside our tent.'

Everyone laughed. A welcome boost, because I was feeling miserable, cold and very, very stiff. Fortunately we nearly had an accident at that point, which meant the conversation about the turd stopped.

The walk on the mud flats was more than four miles, a kind of loop across the flats. We'd end up in Pieterburen, so I wondered what the point was. I mean, we were already in Pieterburen, so we might as well not go walking at all.

The aim of a walk on the mud flats, it turned out, was not to drown. You had to keep moving, otherwise you'd be sucked in and the flats would close in above you. This is where Edwin is going to die, I thought, after I'd walked my first ten yards across the flats. But after half a mile I knew better. It would be me who'd breathe his last. It was so depressing, so pointless, so sad. We even had to swim a short distance, with our clothes on our heads. After three miles I thought, I'll stay here, let myself be sucked down by that slushing, sloshing, sucking, bubbling mass. But someone poked me in the back and I had to keep going. Weeping, I reached Pieterburen.

On the way back to Dwingeloo, I developed a fever. I was given Miss Letty's airbed and sleeping bag, fell asleep and dreamt I hoped I'd never wake up. But I did, from everyone else chanting 'Giethoorn, Giethoorn!' So it was the next day, because that's where we were meant to go. I had to go too. They didn't want to leave me behind on my own. If I stayed at the campsite, everyone else would have to stay back too, so I'd ruin it for everybody else. I felt damp. Giethoorn was a water town. There were no streets, just canals. I wanted to live there. I'd never have to walk with a stick again, there was nowhere to go with a stick. Everyone had to travel by boat. And so we did, we went punting in a gondola. Which meant sticking a pole into the ground and pushing very hard to move forward.

Until there was a thunderstorm.

Then we had to lie down in our gondola. I had never been so frightened. I prayed, please God, let your holy wrath strike our gondola, consume us in a blaze, take us to you.

But the rain stopped, the sun came out and we went for a barbecue.

I felt very ill and threw up my sausage roll, onto a towel. That was the end of it. They were so annoyed with me they immediately rang a taxi, which was to take me straight back to Bussum at the expense of the state. They couldn't have done me a bigger favour than that, I thought when I got into the taxi. But ten minutes later, I changed my mind and asked the driver to go to Dwingeloo, to campsite De Viersprong. I wasn't going to be sent away just like that, I had to prove I could bloody well camp. Luckily, the driver refused. But at least I'd showed courage.

Because all of the Blue Tit was in Dwingeloo, I was temporarily housed at the Blackbird. That was fun right from the start, because they found a bomb. An old bomb from the war, at the Jolly Farmer, whoever he was. He lived at the Huizerweg, close to the petrol pump. All the windows and doors of the Blackbird had to be opened and we weren't allowed to go outside. So there we were, in the sitting area with tea and Mr Willem. Mr Willem was cheerful, it was a shame he didn't work at the Blue Tit. He told us about the pilots. I was going to be a pilot if I couldn't work for the radio, so it was about me too. The pilots had dropped those bombs, but this one hadn't exploded. Now they were going to deactivate it. There was no need for us to be afraid.

I was not afraid. I sat next to Sonja. Sonja was cute. I seesawed with her once, but because she was much heavier than me, it didn't go well. She was fourteen already and in the second class of the Vocational Training School. That's where *I* was going to go the following year. I hoped she'd stay behind a year. A vain hope, because you couldn't repeat a year at our school. Still, I asked her to try it, stay behind a year, and she said she would try her best. We sat hand in hand, waiting for the Jolly Farmer to explode. It was a sweet, warm, slightly sweaty fat hand.

The police rang to say they'd been successful with the bomb. What a shame. I was having such a nice time. The doors and windows were closed again and I had to go to bed, because I still had a fever. How glad I was to be ill. I dreamt of a turd at the Jolly Farmer's. We had to put it on

47

the barbecue to stop it from exploding. But the barbecue sank away in the mud flats, and when the turd exploded, I woke up.

'Oh dear oh dear oh dear,' Miss Trudy said at Play Therapy the next day. My temperature had been taken and it was 98.4, so I had no excuse to stay away.

'Oh dear oh dear oh dear, now what was all that about, my little Otty.'

I was not her 'little Otty'. Besides, my name was Otto.

'I don't know,' I said.

'You got terribly, terribly ill in Dwingeloo.'

I felt a lot better already, but now the colour began to drain from my cheeks again.

'I'm going to get myself a cup of coffee,' she said. 'You go and play with the blocks for a bit, okay?'

She left. I didn't build a tower behind the door. I didn't play. This therapy thing didn't work. When she came back, she asked more questions, but I stayed silent. I didn't talk to immature people like her. She took me on her lap. You didn't do that with eleven-year-olds. It was nice and warm sitting there in her arms with my head leaning against her shoulder and her hand stroking my hair, but I couldn't allow it, because it was *her*. She noticed and let me go.

'Oh well,' she said. 'Go and get the Lego then.'

I got the Lego, built a car with cogs and cheered up because all of them interlocked and turned. Then my Mum rang. She'd had a phone call from Mr Reinier in Dwingeloo.

'What kind of weakling are you?' she yelled angrily. What was I to say to that? I hoped she wouldn't come and pick me up.

'I'm coming to pick you up,' she said, and banged down the phone. I didn't even have time to protest. Just when I was at the Blackbird with Sonja, I had to leave.

She arrived less than half an hour later, Mama Iking, preceded by her perfume. Whenever I heard the loud click-click of her heels on the tiles, I got scared. It sounded like an entire army was marching towards me, a ruthless force that had flattened everything in its path. Then she came through the door. She didn't just open the door, she yanked the handle and threw the door open so violently you'd have been killed instantly if you'd been behind it. Then she'd come up to me, bellow 'Hi!', and kiss me on the forehead. It wasn't a kiss really, it was a shot. The only other thing she needed to do was demand my papers. She always entered the same way, every single time. She sat down and lit a slim cigar. Yes, she did. Now the house was hers. Everywhere she went, every room she entered, was immediately hers. She ruled everything, all the way to the furthest, dustiest corners and cubbyholes where no one ever went. Even the cupboard doors shivered on their hinges when she was there.

'So you were ill,' the interview began.

'Yes.'

'But you don't look ill at all. A little pale, but that's normal for you.'

'I'm better now.'

'No, you're ill. I got a phone call because you're ill. Other people know very well whether you're ill or not.'

I guessed she had to be right. I couldn't look in the mirror to see if I looked healthy at all.

'Say goodbye, because we're going.'

'Yes.'

'Bye.'

I went to look for Sonja and heard my Mum talking to Mr Willem. Oh, she was so very nice all of a sudden, she laughed at his jokes. Mr Willem could make very funny jokes, but so could I, and she never laughed at those. Sonja was in the dormitory.

'You're leaving already?' she said.

'Yes.'

'Shame.'

'Yes.'

'Bye.'

'Bye.'

We sat together, hand in hand, until the order for departure came from downstairs.

'See, you're ill,' my Mum said. 'Your eyes are red.'

Mothers always think they understand everything, but they don't and I didn't ruin her illusions. Discussing it wouldn't help. Everything I dared to put to her was immediately considered contrary, rude and ungrateful. I let her take me to the car and take me to the Princess Margriet Park in Amstelveen.

On the way, my Mum had to suddenly slam on the brakes. 'Stupid bitch!' I heard someone yell. That struck home.

At the Princess Margriet Park, our boxer Vico was very happy to see me. That's what I assumed, at least. It seemed impossible to me that even a dog could be happy about my Mum coming back.

My Dad was there too. He was in his darkroom. The day before he and my Mum had been to a premiere, where he'd taken photographs.

'Don't come in!' he shouted in a worried voice from behind the door when he heard my footsteps on the stairs. He had an odd, very high voice. That was probably why he had no authority at home. Everything he said, even when he was angry, sounded very funny. That's why I liked him.

'No, Dad,' I said in as low a voice as I could. My voice was lower now than his even though it hadn't broken yet. Perhaps it never would. I worried about that sometimes. A voice like that was probably hereditary.

My room wasn't a room, it was a cupboard with a bed, a table, a chair and a little radio. The rest of my things were at the Institute. I sat down on my bed and turned on the radio. The first thing I heard was '*I do everything for Sonja*', a pathetic song by Rob de Nijs, but it was about Sonja. Which was no coincidence, they'd put it on especially for me because they just knew I'd turn on my radio at that very moment. Oh... it wasn't for me after all.

It was for the workers at the De Koning & Sons tin factory in Lopik. I guessed they must have known about Sonja and me and planned to call them to thank them.

'Would you like to join me for a bit in the darkroom?'

I hadn't heard my Dad come into the room. He always opened doors very quietly, probably to spare them, for my Mum.

He had a beard, my Dad, which tickled when he kissed me.

'Sure,' I said.

My Dad used me as an assistant in the darkroom, because I could find my way around better in there than he could. I liked spending time there, it was the best room in the house. My Dad spoke differently in the dark. He pronounced every sentence as if he was telling a secret, a bit like Reverend van Kampen at Sunday school. My Mum was afraid in the darkroom. She should be there all day, really. We weren't scared, we did our work and had good conversations. He told me about the premiere of the play he'd seen the day before, at the Amstelveen Cultural Centre.

'It couldn't have been better,' he said. 'Your Mum made the actors' costumes and I took photographs of them. So if there are any flaws in the clothes, I can touch them up so they'll still look beautiful in the newspaper.'

He laughed out loud. Me too. Not that I had any idea what he meant, but it was funny because my Dad was laughing.

'Try and be nice to your Mum,' he said. 'She's lost her job.'

Be nice to my Mum? It had never struck me there could be such a thing, but I would be, or try to be, at least. Then she called us from downstairs, the order being, 'Tea!'

'I'll just finish this,' my Dad said. 'You go ahead. And remember, be nice.'

'Here,' she said, and she pressed a biscuit into my hand. 'Your tea is right in front of you.'

'Gee, Mum,' I said, 'so you're unemployed.'

'Who told you that?'

'Dad.'

'Yes, they don't want me any more. My clothes aren't good enough.'

I could imagine that. I always had to wear jumpers and trousers with patches sewn onto the elbows and knees. I even had a pair of trousers that was too short. My Mum cut off the trouser legs, put strips of leather on them and then reattached the bits of fabric she had cut off. Even at the Institute they laughed at people who wore trousers like that.

I understood, but I had to be nice, so I said, 'How awful for you.'

'Bah, don't be so dramatic.'

I was still learning to be nice.

'I'm going out with Sonja.'

'With Sonja? What the heck do you see in *her*, that podgy little thing?'

As if I wasn't worth a podgy little thing.

'You can make our clothes when we get married.'

I think I must have done something wrong, for something terrible happened. Something I'd never witnessed before. My Mum burst into tears. The General herself was crying! I froze in my chair. What was I to do? Fortunately my Dad came down. I jumped up and went out into the garden to check if the bikes were still in the shed.

'Otto!' said a voice on the other side of the fence.

'Kas!'

'Wrong, it's Koos.'

Kas and Koos were the neighbours' twins. Their voices sounded exactly alike. They didn't look alike, but that was no use to me. They were eleven too, like me.

'Shall we go to the sea of sand?' I asked.

'Good idea,' Koos said.

He took me on the back of his bike. The sea of sand was a dirty, muddy field with a smelly puddle in the middle – a kind of mini mud flat, but nice and exciting.

'Cigarette?' Koos said.

'Yes, please.' I wanted to sound experienced, but I could hear my voice quaver ridiculously.

'The other way,' said Koos, 'the filter isn't for lighting.'

I smoked, but my lungs refused to let the smoke in. 'It's a matter of practice,' said Koos. 'I can inhale.'

Ha, that was easy for him to say, I couldn't check that. We cycled back home with our mouths open, otherwise our parents would know we'd been smoking.

'Had a nice smoke?' my Dad asked.

'I didn't smoke.'

'Yes, you did, chappy. I saw you cycling with your mouth open and I thought, aha, he must have been smoking. If you stop, I'll give you an ice lolly.'

I stopped immediately. My Mum was asleep in her chair. She woke up when dinner was ready. My Dad did the cooking and he cooked really well. She slurped her soup off her spoon and then I knew – she was woozy. She was always woozy when I came. She drank 'little sherries', which made her talk funny. She always said the same things on those evenings. That she'd have liked to be an artist, but that she wasn't one because she'd had me. She said it now.

'What a pity,' I said. I had to be nice, after all.

'A pity, a *pity*? It's bloody awful! Awful, you hear!'

She was shouting at that point. Soup splattered against my face. Oh, if only I were with the podgy little thing at the Institute, I thought.

'Calm down, sweetheart,' my Dad said.

'Keep out of it, jerk. You and your squeaky voice!'

I'd heard it so many times before. Now she was going to talk about the war and the camps, and about how all the Germans ought to be lined up against the wall and shot. And we'd say we agreed, because that made her happy. Then everything would be fine until something else came up she could argue about. And yes, no sooner was the soup

53

finished and the Germans dead than the Chinese had to take the rap. We had noodles for dinner. The Chinese too had to be lined up against the wall and shot.

'You need quite a long wall for that,' I said.

'Well, they've got one, haven't they? The Great Wall of China.'

So much for the Chinese. There were no further casualties during dinner, apart from the football supporters, who were liquidated, and the arms dealers, who needed to be wiped out with their own merchandise.

My Dad did the dishes, made coffee and talked softly, worried that he might wake my now harmless Mum – which would have had terrible consequences for all the nations in the world.

What is sherry? I wondered. It did something funny to you. It made you very angry when you drank it, and it made you snore and throw shoes. At least, that's what my Mum did when my Dad woke her up thinking she'd be more comfortable in bed. She always threw my Dad's shoes. He wore size 11, so it was hard to miss anything, but she always did.

The next day my Mum was a shadow of the tyrant she'd been the day before. She was quiet and kept touching me. She said strange things: that she loved me and wanted me to live at home. I'd never heard her say that before. Had she been drinking sherry again? I didn't think so because she said it differently, not like the evening before but softer and in a low, dreamy voice full of long-drawn-out words. Then she began to cry and her hands shook, spilling tea onto mine. Everything was a failure, she said, her life, Dad's life, my life, her career, everything. It was all pointless, empty and pointless. What was the use of having a sandwich, of pouring another cup of tea? Soon the whole breakfast table would need to be cleared again. By her. And why? Tomorrow morning all those stupid things would be back – the ridiculous teapot, the stupid bread basket, the pathetic jar of peanut butter with that insufferably irritating sun on the lid, the cheese box that smelled of old socks, the rusk tin you could never open, those shabby wooden plates on which so many sandwiches had been buttered, which only kept you alive. And what for? For what purpose? Only so she could put that junk here again tomorrow, and the day after, and the day after that. Only so she could spread the sun on a sandwich and be unable to open the rusk tin again. And that horrible man with his annoying, squeaky voice and his grubby beard. As always, he'd come slowly creaking down the stairs in his slippers, sit down goddamn cheerfully and rub his hands together – so annoying. No one had ever understood her. Only Vico came close. She liked him licking her bare toes, it was comforting. When he sat on the doormat and scratched the door to indicate that he needed to go out, she waited until he began to howl and bark. Then she'd open the door and he'd run out, have a crap in the park and come back to thank her. She didn't have such a bond with humans. Not even with that happy, slipper-shod sod. Him and his eternal whistling. He was always whistling, even during fights, during sex, at funerals. Not a minute went by without that shrill, stupid noise. She often dreamt she punched his teeth out to be rid of that whistling, but she had neither the courage nor the strength for it. She didn't have the courage or strength for anything any more, so she just sat there with her tea and her tears. Which had just run out when he came creaking down the stairs – in his slippers, oh yes. He sat down and began to read out the newspaper headlines. That too was a daily ritual. There was never anything new about the news, particularly his.

Then Mum got a grip on herself. She said that I was going to finish primary school that summer. Which I knew, of course, she didn't have to tell me so solemnly. She and my Dad were thinking that it might be good for me to go to a regular school, where I'd join regular children. It all seemed very regular to me. She was looking forward, she said, to looking after me, especially now that it didn't look like she was going to get work anytime soon. My Dad read the paper and whistled. I couldn't ask him what my Mum and he meant by it all, because he wasn't to be disturbed at such moments.

'But,' she said, 'first I'll go on holiday.'

'Oh, where are we going?'

'You're not coming and neither is your father.'

She said it in a serious tone, so it probably wasn't going to be a cheerful holiday. Perhaps she was planning to go to Dwingeloo.

'I'm going to the Veluwe for a while,' she said sadly.

She left that same afternoon and cried when she was saying goodbye. My Dad had to explain everything. We went up to the darkroom and he began.

'She's going on a holiday,' he said, 'to learn not to drink sherry any more.'

He sounded very nervous, not like he usually did in the darkroom. Was the light still on?

'She can't,' he said, 'she's not... Well, she finds it difficult to keep away from the bottle, so she needs to unlearn it there. They're going to teach her.'

Was that all? Why was he making such a fuss about that? All he needed to do was hide the bottle.

'No,' he said, 'it's not that easy. She'll find another bottle.'

It's true my Mum always found everything. I could never keep any birthday presents hidden from her, no matter how well I hid them.

'How long will it take, the unlearning?' I asked.

He sighed and remained silent.

'You need to go back to the Institute tomorrow,' he said finally. 'I need to go back to work.'

The rest of the day was great. First we went for a ride on the tandem. We raced Zoetemelk and Van Impe all the way to the traffic lights, leaving them far behind us. The lights were red. That's where they caught up with us. I don't think the lights were red at all, I didn't hear any cars. I think my Dad just made it up because he wanted to stop. He had no stamina. After the cycle ride we went for dinner at an Italian restaurant, and in the evening there was football. My Dad did the commentary. He was brilliant at it.

On the way to Bussum the following day, we talked about mainstream school.

'It'll be much more fun for you,' he said, 'among sighted children.'

I doubted it. Children are children, whether they can see or not. I told him of my decision, because I'd taken a decision that night.

'I'll only do it,' I said, 'if Mum is never woozy again.'

He didn't answer and we drove into the car park.

Dear Reverend van Kampen,

My parents want me to come and live with them next year. I'll have finished primary school, and they think I should attend a mainstream school. I'm supposed to really like this. I will finally be delivered from those awful blind kids, I will be able to take part in normal society, but I don't dare. Not because of the school, I'm sure I'll manage. No, it's because of something else altogether. The atmosphere at home is awful. My Mum drinks a lot of sherry when I'm there. Last night I witnessed something terrible. I couldn't sleep because my parents were shouting at each other. I went downstairs to support my father. He was desperate. 'But I love you!' he yelled, with a catch in his high-pitched voice. And my Mum kept saying, 'I want to be dead, I want to be dead.' When my Dad saw me standing by the door, he began to cry. We went upstairs. He took me to my room and said I should try and get some sleep. Then I heard him fetch my Mum and, with great difficulty, he managed to get her to bed. This has happened a lot, Reverend, and I don't want to go to mainstream school.

They were all back: Walter, the Snail, Edwin and all those other happy campers. They were still excited and, like parrots, kept repeating the details of the variety show the day before. Not once, but hundreds of times, and each time it sounded crazier than before. My story about the bomb was lost in the din. Only Pieter heard.

'That lousy bomb of yours didn't even explode,' he said. 'But we fished for Coke.'

Fishing for Coke, an utterly ridiculous invention. I'd done it myself once, so it wasn't new to me. Someone put a bottle of Coke on the ground, then you needed to find the cap of the bottle with a magnet on a string. If you caught one, you could reel it in and drink the Coke.

'And we Tomadoed!' Walter shouted.

Another really sad thing. You got into a Tomado storage box on wheels and pulled yourself forward along a piece of string that the staff had strung up. What fun. No one asked what I'd done. It didn't matter. I didn't have anything to tell them that they'd understand.

I walked over to the Blackbird to see Sonja. She was doing homework, something I longed to do. At the Vocational Training School you had to learn lecture notes by heart. She was studying Maxwell's corkscrew rule. 'If you put your right hand into an imaginary conductor...' The bit about it being imaginary was very important. It was underlined. As if some stupid blind kid might get it into his thick skull to really do that! If you could recite the notes without making a mistake, they punched a hole in your to-do list. When you got eighteen holes, the list was full and you were given a new one. Maxwell was hole number four, so there was quite a lot left to learn.

'Hello, podgy little thing,' I said cheerfully.

It took me eight minutes and eleven seconds to convince her that I didn't know that that wasn't a nice thing to say.

'You don't need to repeat a year,' I said. 'If everything goes according to plan, I'm going to mainstream school next year.'

'Oh,' she said. 'In that case you can test me.'

She handed me her Braille book, which had very flattened dots in it. It had to be hard, pushing all those dots into your head. Besides Maxwell, we did Volt, Ampere, Ohm and Watt. Then she'd had enough of it. Five holes, that's all the physicists were going to get that day.

'Aren't you happy?' Sonja asked.

'Why?'

'Well, because you're allowed to go to mainstream school.'

I said what I heard Prime Minister Den Uyl say on the radio the other day. 'Yes and no.'

'I'd love it,' she said, 'but I'm not ready for it.'

That's what her foster parents had decided, in consultation with the Institute. Sonja didn't have real parents, they were dead. They'd been dead for a very long time, so she didn't mind. The next day her foster parents were coming to pick her up. She was going to ask them about mainstream school again, but the chances of her being allowed to go were very slim. What the Institute said was sacred.

The Institute hadn't decided about me yet. They might just foil my mother's plans. It was complete nonsense, by the way, the Institute deciding whether we were ready for mainstream school. Seeing children weren't told whether they were ready for mainstream school, were they? Perhaps I wasn't ready for it. The next day I was probably going to have a preliminary meeting with Mr Hak about it. That was the dream of every blind person, mainstream school. The blind thought sighted people were nice. And sometimes they were, but they could be very cruel too. Sometimes, when we played football in the park near my parents' house, I walked into the barbed wire and they laughed their heads off. I'd beat them up then. Which was fine when there were just three of them, but it wouldn't be if there was an entire *class* of sighted kids. The Institute might be full of imbeciles, but it had one advantage:

everyone was equal.

Since it was time for our evening sandwiches, I went back to the Blue Tit, because they were expecting me. There was something new on the menu, sandwich spread. I'd heard about it, and had asked Mum to buy it, but she said it looked like vomit. Here, that didn't make a difference. I only wanted sandwich spread but first we had to have two sandwiches with a savoury topping, like cheese or ham. Only then we could have something sweet. Sandwich spread wasn't sweet, but it still counted as sweet.

Harry was back. It took me ten minutes to discover that, because Mr Reinier asked for silence.

'Harry,' he said, 'has something rather unpleasant to tell you.'

I thought about his eyes, and about how much of a dick I was as far as Harry was concerned. He still thought I'd stolen them, and now he was probably going to tell everyone at the Blue Tit.

'My sister...' Harry began.

What did his sister have to do with it?

'My sister has been taken hostage.'

Taken hostage? That was new.

'By South Moluccans.'

South Moluccans? They were new to me too. Taken hostage by South Moluccans. I waited for an explanation, yet none was given. No one understood, but we were all quiet because when Harry said something in a voice like that, it was something terrible. Even cheeky Walter didn't say a word. Then Mr Reinier explained. He told us about Doctor Manusama and about the free Republic of the Moluccas, which the South Moluccans wanted. However, no one else wanted it, which was why they'd taken Harry's sister hostage, to press their demands. Because Harry's sister was at school, and they'd attacked the school with guns. No one was allowed to leave. That's what hostage-taking was about. She was at a mainstream school. In that case you were asking for it at least a little, for being taken hostage. It would be better for me to stay at the Institute. Here you didn't run that risk. It was sad for Harry, he was very quiet because of it all. But I was relieved, because now he didn't have an eye for his eyes.

After dinner I climbed into the pain tree, which was in the middle of the field, beside the seesaw. It was called the pain tree because all the blind kids bumped into it quite often. But the pain tree was the only place where you could be on your own, which you couldn't be anywhere else, not even in the loo. After five minutes, Miss Kootje would come and tell you to *squeeze* it. I sat on my branch hatching a plan. Tomorrow I'd take the linen-room lady hostage, because I wanted a free and independent Institute. Harry came and climbed up too. I kept very quiet, but he could smell me. My Mum used a washing detergent that no one else would ever want to use.

'I really didn't have your eyes,' I said.

'I know,' Harry said indifferently. 'It was Edwin.'

He clearly wasn't worried about his eyes, only about his sister.

'We need to free her,' he said.

'But how?'

'We smash down the doors of the school with Van Halen's cart and then we kill the South Moluccans.'

It sounded like a good plan. But how were we to get the cart to Bovensmilde, which was where the school was? Ah yes, with Mr Reinier's moped! I could drive it really well. We could tie the cart to the rear carrier, and Harry could sit in the cart. One had to do something to free one's sister. We'd kill the South Moluccans by siphoning petrol into a container, setting it alight and throwing it over the South Moluccans. The plan was watertight, we'd leave that very night. There'd be enough room left in the cart for bread and eight jars of sandwich spread. We had one small problem though. We didn't know where Van Halen left the cart after he'd taken dinner around. It used to be parked in front of the Blue Tit, but after the accident it was being kept somewhere else. We walked over to the soup kitchen, because we knew where that was. But the cart wasn't there. What we did find was a car. Perhaps we could go by car? But the car was locked. We looked outside the printing office and the main building, but we didn't find the cart. So we decided to ring Van Halen's doorbell.

'Yes?' Van Halen shouted through the intercom.

'Hi Jan,' Harry said in as deep a voice as he could manage. 'Hi Jan, it's Frits, the chef. I need the cart for a minute, because I need to take some food around. Where did you put it?'

'Buzz off, Harry,' Van Halen shouted from the open window above us. We decided to wait until the next day and work out how we could get the cart when Van Halen took the food round. It would be difficult, but we'd do anything for Harry's sister. We also needed to check if Mr Reinier would be on duty, because of the moped. I asked him before we went to bed.

'Yes,' he said, 'from two in the afternoon till ten at night.'

'Gee,' I said, 'that's nice.'

'I beg your pardon! Do you think that's nice?'

We needed a compass to find Bovensmilde. There was a Braille one in Mr Hak's classroom, so we needed to steal it, and there was only one way of getting Hak to leave the classroom.

'Mr Hak?' I asked him the following morning.

'Yes, Ottoman, tell me, boy.'

'Do you think I'm ready for mainstream school?'

'Well, my friend,' he said solemnly, 'I'd be happy to talk to you about it, but not here. Come to my office. Harry, could you look after the little ones for a minute?'

'Sure Mr Hak, I'll keep an eye on them,' Harry said.

Hak liked nothing better than sitting in his office and looking important.

'Take a seat,' he said, 'take a seat.'

He began to smoke right away, that's what you did in an office.

'So you were asking about mainstream school, son. Well, the able-bodied world can be very tough.'

Meanwhile I heard the noise in the classroom next door grow increasingly loud. Crash! That was cheeky Walter dropping his desk lid. Bang! That was the Snail. As soon as Hak left the classroom, Hajo started rocking his chair, falling over backwards with it.

'Children will always find it hard to accept that you're different.'

Thud! Someone threw a Braille book on the floor.

'Whatever's different, people find strange.'

'Aaargh!' A blood-curdling scream from Marja. She'd been kicked by Edwin.

'You must realise that you need to compensate for your lack of sight in one way or another...'

Kaboom! An enormous bang, even the floor in the office shook. Hak jumped up. I quietly walked after him, back to the classroom. The cupboard with stereo equipment had fallen over. That meant no more school radio for the time being. I still didn't know whether I was ready for regular school or not, but it didn't matter. Harry had had enough time to steal the compass.

'Do you know how the compass works, by the way?' Hak asked after the last pieces of the radio had been swept up.

'Oh yes,' Harry and I said together.

'Yes?'

'Yes,' I said, 'the needle points at the magnetic North and gets confused when there is too much steel nearby, because it's pulled in all directions.'

'I'll get the compass,' Hak said, and then the bell rang.

Harry didn't understand how the compass worked and gave it to me while we walked to the Blue Tit.

It was fifteen degrees.

It was the thermometer.

So we'd have to find Bovensmilde without a compass. If we'd had one, we'd only have had to head north, because that's where Bovensmilde was. Now we'd have to ask where the north was. We'd ask at the petrol pump. We needed to go there anyway, to fill up the moped.

During the milk break we heard that there was no news about Harry's sister. The situation was unchanged.

When we were back in Mr Hak's classroom, he began to talk about the compass again and wanted to show us how it worked, but the compass was gone. So, was the thermometer the compass, after all? Hak went to look for it. First he went to see year one, two and three. They were one class too, so that was done very quickly. Then he checked at the Vocational Training School and the Junior Technical School, but he couldn't find the compass.

Next, the cart. That was going to be more difficult. Van Halen's dinner delivery ended at the Wagtail. Harry would follow him there. He would be suffering from diarrhoea so wouldn't have to eat with the rest. He'd start a conversation with Hak and keep him talking until they reached the place where he parked the cart these days. Meanwhile I would also have been excused from having dinner due to a sudden and serious bout of the runs. I was going to put my linen-room plan into action as part of our preparations for the mission in Bovensmilde.

I had loaded my pistol. It wasn't a pistol, really, but a gun. You needed to slide a round with eight tiny bombs onto the cylinder.

'I demand a free and independent Institute!' I shouted when I threw the door open.

'Hi,' the linen-room ladies said. 'Would you like some liquorice, Otto?'

'No liquorice, a free and independent Institute! I mean it this time!'

'A kitty or a farmhouse?'

'A kitten liquorice, please.'

I dropped my weapon. Why would you want to be free

and independent if you could have liquorice? I'd buy a bag for the South Moluccans at the pump tonight.

The log cabin had become the control room. I waited there for Harry, who came to tell me that he'd failed to get the cart. Van Halen had sent him away.

I was to have a Mantoux that afternoon. It sounded a bit suspicious, but it was a tuberculosis test.

'Watch out,' Nurse Pauka cried when I was about to enter the clinic. 'Watch out, or you'll bump into Van Halen's cart.'

Thank goodness for tuberculosis.

There were only two jars of sandwich spread left, so I added a jar of sun-lidded peanut butter from the pantry. There was Swiss cheese too, but that was dangerous, because it would give away the attack plan before we even got there. There was also half a loaf of Kingcorn – brown or white, I didn't know.

Mr Reinier was playing the guitar. If he was singing 'The House of the Rising Sun', you could do anything, so we pulled the moped off its stand and walked to the clinic with it. We put the food in the cart and I tied the cart to the rear carrier of the moped with a piece of string. We were going to walk to the petrol pump. That's where we could get petrol for three guilders and twenty cents. That's all we had. We had to make it with that. Harry held his stick in his left hand and pushed me with his right. I didn't have any hands free, because I had to use both to steer the moped. The cart kept bumping into the rear carrier, but with Harry in it that surely wouldn't happen. We didn't have money for a bag of liquorice, but I'd kept a piece from the linen-room. We walked past the reception, through the gate, turned right, walked down the service road, crossed it at the flyover over the motorway and crossed the flyover. Then we turned left, to where the petrol pump was.

Inside the shop, the radio was blaring.

'Which pump?' the man behind the counter shouted.

'No pump,' I yelled. 'Could you fill up our moped?'

The music on the radio was interrupted for an extra news bulletin.

'The Moluccan hostage-takers at the school in Bovensmilde freed all children at around seven thirty this evening. The children are safe. Several teachers are still being kept hostage.'

'Never mind,' I said. 'No petrol. I'll have a packet of Camels, please.'

'Three fifty,' the man said.

That was a shame. I was thirty cents short.

We weren't really happy when we walked back. Harry's sister was free, but not because of us. Our carefully prepared mission was off. We weren't going to free the teachers, that'd be a waste of time. They could be sacrificed to the free and independent Republic of the South Moluccas. No one ever knew about our plan, but Van Halen smelled of sandwich spread for days.

That evening Radio Fed Up broadcast an extensive interview with Harry H, the relieved brother of one of the hostages of the mainstream school in Bovensmilde.

The following day we were visited by a reporter from the AVRO broadcasting corporation. He wanted to make a school radio programme about what it was like to be blind, which we apparently knew all about. Hak did most of the talking.

'The able-bodied world can be very tough.'

It sounded even more official because it was being recorded. I dropped my braillewriter on the floor. The recording had to be done again. My oh my, what rubbish Hak talked. It would all have to be cut from the programme. It should have been about us, but this was about Hak. Then it was Harry's turn. He had to cycle for the radio, pour coffee, and run, and the reporter was amazed.

'Incredible!' he kept saying into his microphone.

There was nothing to it, but Harry was very proud of himself. Stupid. Who demonstrates that he can pour coffee for the radio? I'd never do that, but then again I hadn't been asked to pour coffee. I was asked to talk about my transmitter, though. The school radio man said it was 'exceedingly interesting'.

'Yes,' he said. 'If you're not that mobile, like Otto here, you start looking for other ways to express yourself.'

Not that mobile? If only he knew about Bovensmilde, but I couldn't tell him about that on the radio. Then he asked something odd. Whether I missed my parents sometimes. I didn't know how to answer that.

I couldn't sleep that night. I listened to the sound of the motorway, the sound of the trucks whizzing along. There is no lonelier sound than that.

For three days we had a lot of media attention. The next day, a television crew came to visit. *Sports Panorama* came to film us doing gymnastics. This time Mooyman was confident enough to play the piano, but he'd made a deal with the director before he began. If he sounded terrible, they'd use a tune by Pim Jacobs to accompany the images of the jogging blind. I imagined a star role for myself, but things worked out differently. Jumping over the cord, I took a nose dive. That was filmed. And broadcast. And repeated in slow motion with a voice-over.

'It doesn't always go well. Look at what happened to eleven-year-old Otto Iking...'

'Here's the repeat. We see the run-up, the one moment of hesitation, the left foot snagging on the cord, and the inevitable impact with the very hard floor...'

'Again, that fatal run-up...'

This went on for another two minutes. Uncle Jan, the taxi driver, saw it too.

'Hey, TV star!' he said with a smile. 'I've never seen anyone nose-dive so beautifully.'

Bloody AVRO. They even won a prize with it at some festival. When the camera crew had left and I was being treated by Nurse Pauka, the radio man returned. He'd forgotten to record something. Harry on a horse.

The school radio programme was broadcast a week later. A week could be very long, and this one was. Fifteen degrees and partly cloudy every day, the same trucks on the motorway every night and no news from my parents. When I rang my Dad at the Princess Margriet Park, he didn't answer the phone and I didn't have my Mum's number. Radio Fed Up had little information, just music, Jack Jersey's 'Papa was a Poor Man'.

Then, inevitably, the day of the school radio broadcast came. We were given time off to listen to it because we didn't have a new radio in the classroom yet. The insurance company didn't want to pay up. Not surprisingly. They knew only too well the kind of nonsense that set usually produced. There was absolutely no point in paying damages for it. So we listened at the Blue Tit, but it was Hak this and Harry that. I didn't feature at all, they only played a silly song by John Denver that was broadcast by Radio Fed Up and the theme song of the Otto Show, a recording of me playing the alto flute. This called for revenge. I decided to use the Jostikit to make listening to the AVRO impossible from then on. The following night AVRO's *Sports Panorama* featured the film of us doing gymnastics. We didn't have television at the Blue Tit.

Harry began to act like a star. The super blind made no secret about being super blind. He had been at the 'editoring' of the school radio show.

'The editing, you mean,' I said.

'What do you know about it, nose diver?'

I didn't know anything about it, but I did know the meaning of the word editing. Harry was a star, he'd already had an offer from the gossip magazine *Privé*. Killing two birds with one stone, they wanted to interview him, his parents and his sister. They could talk about being taken hostage *and* about being blind, super blind in Harry's case. His success went to his head. Suddenly he refused to make coffee for the staff, as he'd proved on the radio that he could do it. Now he left the job to lesser children like me.

Neither was he supplying any Institute news for Radio Fed Up any more, because he was waiting for a big offer from a broadcasting corporation.

Someone called for me. That didn't happen very often. I hoped it was my Dad, but it was someone else, unfortunately, a colleague of the radio reporter. He'd heard the show, and he thought it was wonderful that I had my own transmitter. How did he know? That wasn't broadcast at all.

'No,' he said, 'but I was there during the editing of the programme.'

He wanted to come and talk to me. He'd explain during his visit. Tomorrow he had time, he said. Me too, I always had time. He'd come to Mr Hak's classroom at four o'clock. I'd ask Hak whether we could use his office. It was the only place where we could talk without being bothered by blind morons.

'Who was that?' Harry asked.

'Oh, someone from the radio.'

'But I was here!'

'He didn't call to talk to you, Harry, he wanted to talk to me.'

'Oh sure, he probably made a complaint about the fact that we can never listen to the AVRO here because of that Jostikit of yours.'

'No, he said he wants to come and talk to me.'

'He'll come and confiscate that transmitter, mark my words.'

I had recently built a wooden box during art class with a padlock on it. Miss Emmie, the art teacher, called it 'Pandora's box'. I put the Jostikit in it and padlocked it. To be on the safe side, I didn't air the Otto Show that night.

'You've come to see one of my pupils?' I heard Hak ask in the corridor.

I couldn't hear the answer, because at that point Walter began to imitate Harry Nak, one of comedian André van Duin's characters who was even more popular than Van Duin himself.

Hak called me to his office. When Hak was leaving, he said to the visitor, 'Keep an eye on him, he interrupts your

71

programmes.'

The man from the AVRO introduced himself as Kees and told me to call him that without the Mr bit. He thought it completely unnecessary to be formal.

'Okay, Kees,' I said, feeling blood rushing to my cheeks.

Kees was from The Hague. He had a funny accent that I'd never heard before. He worked for the youth department of the AVRO. They had been thinking about making some youth programmes presented by young people. Because I was doing so well with my transmitter, demonstrating I was really interested in the medium, and because I had a good voice – he really said that – Kees thought it was a good idea to make a test recording with me as the presenter. They had considered Harry, but they thought his accent was too provincial.

Kees had brought a tape recorder, so we could record me reading a bit of text that he could play to the other members of the editorial staff. I got my braillewriter from the classroom and Kees dictated a text about Boy Scouts. I read it out, talking into the microphone. I wasn't as fluent as the listeners of Radio Fed Up were used to, but I wasn't dissatisfied.

'Okay,' Kees said. 'That background noise, though, what's that?'

'That's my fingers on the sheet of Braille paper.'

I read the text again, this time with the piece of paper on my lap under the table. Kees went back to Hilversum, saying he'd be in touch.

Talking into a Radio Fed Up microphone that night I announced my forthcoming move to the AVRO. But Fed Up would continue, that was certain. I was just going to stop interrupting the AVRO broadcasts for a while.

Harry wasn't in the dormitory studio during the broadcast; no one knew where he was. Just after I got to bed, I heard him enter through the fire escape. He fell on his bed and began to talk funny, the way my Mum did after she had drunk sherry. He had probably been to the Beat Cellar. The Beat Cellar was an underground space for older blind kids who were allowed to drink beer. Apparently they had sherry too. Harry went there every week. He'd even shagged someone there, or so he claimed. I went with him once. Everyone was smoking, including the Snail, who was there too. He had a cigarette which he puffed at for five minutes before someone with bad eyesight told him it wasn't lit. They danced to loud music in the Beat Cellar and every thirty seconds or so someone bumped into the record player, so they had to start the record again. I didn't like the Beat Cellar, and I didn't notice any shagging.

The following morning Hak was very nervous. He'd received a shipment of East German demonstration materials the day before and today was the day for... sex education. We were going to be taught with rubber models from behind the Iron Curtain. Hak opened the boxes and made puzzled hissing sounds.

'Everyone will get a set of genitalia on their table,' Hak began. 'Of course you all know what you have yourself.'

He sounded like my Dad in the darkroom, talking about my Mum's holiday to the Veluwe. I had a willy, so I got one on my table. That and another thing which girls had, a vagina. The willy consisted of a rubber pipe. It smelled like the bicycle repair shop. At the end of the pipe was a small ball which could be squeezed, just like the one on the horn of my go-cart. When you squeezed the ball, the willy grew. You could make it shrivel up by taking a cap off the willy. The vagina was a triangular thing with flaps. So that was what girls had between their legs. There were bits of fuzz on it too, just like around the willy. What was that for? That wasn't what the real thing was like, I didn't have any fuzz. I guessed that the East Germans liked decorating the willies and vaginas.

'If the man,' said Hak, 'feels like having sex, his penis grows bigger. Pump up the penises, guys.'

We happily squeezed the horn balls.

'Right. And if the woman feels like it, the flaps will open slowly, creating space for the penis in the hole between the flaps. Open up the flaps and put the penis inside.'

And so we did.

'Then the penis moves up and down in the hole and, at some point, produces sperm.'

The phone rang. While Hak was on it, we moved our penises up and down inside the vaginas and waited for a miracle. The rubber squeaked. The person at the other end of the line must have been able to hear it because Hak said, 'We're making music.'

I thought I felt sperm coming out of the penis on my table, but it was my own sweat, it had made my hands damp. Hak hung up.

'Stop for a minute, people. So then the sperm comes out...'

He said 'sperm', but I thought it was 'spern'. I'd heard the Snail talk about spern.

'Then the sperm goes into the hole and deep inside the hole is an egg waiting.'

He talked faster and faster.

'Then a seed from the sperm attaches itself to the egg and then you get a baby.'

Phew, that was it. He sighed with relief.

'Is that what shagging is about?' Harry asked.

He betrayed himself. So he hadn't shagged anyone in the Beat Cellar.

'Where did you hear that word?' Hak asked.

'My father said it.'

Harry's father was a farmer.

'It's true that some people use the word that you just used, but it's not very polite. We prefer to talk about making love, going to bed with someone or having intercourse, that's better.' So we decided to say 'shag', because everything Hak considered impolite was good.

'Okay, let the air out of the penises, guys.'

We pulled the caps off and the penises deflated. The communist genitalia were then returned to their boxes and we had milk.

'We shagged with East German willies!' Pieter yelled.

He was jumping up and down. Miss Kootje got angry. She was jealous. She forbade us to use 'that word', as she called it. If we did, we were to pay five cents per offence. That's how I spent all my pocket money shagging. I just couldn't stop doing it. I couldn't help myself.

I thought long and hard in the pain tree and came to the conclusion that the supercalifragilisticexpialidocious feeling in my willy had to have something to do with that sperm, or spern. While I'd been in the bath with my duck, it had felt like I almost needed to pee. If I'd been allowed to stay in that bath any longer with my duck against my willy, I'd have peed spern or sperm, and if there had been a vagina behind it, I'd have produced a baby. I got an idea. What a duck could do, my hand should be able to do too. I rubbed, and I felt my willy grow bigger. A miracle. I continued doing that until I had that great feeling again. It was better than ever. I didn't dare rub for very long, because I wouldn't get clean underwear until the next day. Still, I'd made a very important discovery.

Kees from the radio called. It was okay. Okay, Kees. They'd asked fifteen other children to read out texts, and had chosen me. I was to be the presenter of the new youth programme. It was going to start next week, the very next week. Tomorrow I needed to go to the AVRO by taxi to meet the other members of the editorial staff. Ha! What would Harry think of that? With his cycling and horse riding and making coffee on the radio. That kind of showing off didn't get you anywhere, it was all about your voice, and the AVRO didn't want yokels. All yokels could do was talk about shagging in a funny accent.

'We've been screwed by *Privé*!' Harry yelled the next day. See, there it was again. He didn't get punished for it, because you weren't punished yet for saying 'screw', but that would certainly change, because it was an increasingly popular word.

'Yes,' I said. 'They're parasites.'

That's what I heard my father say. *Privé* had once published some of his photographs without his permission.

'No,' cheeky Walter said, 'mushrooms are parasites.'

He had been paying attention during our biology class.

'They're morons,' Harry yelled. 'Sons of bitches.'

Mr Reinier tried to calm him down, but failed. Harry kicked the cupboards, banged the doors and went to the dormitory, swearing. The silence that followed was more silent than at other times when there was nothing to hear. The only thing I could hear was the whistling of the wind in the pain tree. Mr Reinier told us what had happened. *Privé* had published the interview with Harry, his sister and his parents, but the article wasn't very nice. He read it out to us.

When Truus Klokma and Henk Hazels said 'I will' to each other at the town hall of Beilen on the 21st of June 1964, it was a beautiful day. Nothing stood in the way of their marital bliss. A year later Truus proudly gave birth to a six-and-a-half-pound baby boy, Harry. Their second child, Rita, nearly five pounds, arrived soon after. However, a year after her birth their happy dream was dashed. Harry developed a tumour, which made him lose sight in both his eyes. He has lived in Bussum ever since, in the residential section of the Institute for the Blind. They're trying to educate him there as best they can. It's a matter of trial and error, but where there's a will, there's a way. It's still very hard for Truus and Henk Hazels, but they had no choice. Raising a blind child at home, without the necessary expert guidance, is impossible. Less than two weeks ago, the unfortunate Hazels were struck by another disaster. Their daughter Rita was taken hostage during her geography class. How much can a family bear? We asked those involved.

76

This was followed by the interview with Harry, Rita and their parents. The whole thing was wrong, their words had been twisted and they had been made to sound as pathetic as possible.

Harry's father rang. He was so angry, you could hear him shout everywhere in the Blue Tit. Harry didn't want to talk to him. Then the taxi arrived to take me to the AVRO. It was Uncle Jan again.

'So you're going on the radio?' he said. 'Well, at least no one will see you take a nose dive over a cord.'

I let him rabbit on.

The name of my programme was *Otto's Slate Corner*. Kees, Claudia and Piet came up with that. Kees, Claudia and Piet were the editorial staff. The idea was that we'd discuss things that adults had invented for children and completely slate them. The first broadcast was to deal with scouting. That's what we did at the Institute too. Every Wednesday afternoon we were visited by a mobile Scout mistress. I joined her troupe once. We had to say '*dop dop dop, arf arf arf*'. That was just so childish, it deserved to be trashed on the radio. I thought it was a very good idea, but maybe I had an even better plan for the first *Otto's Slate Corner*. I suggested talking about Harry's interview with *Privé*. They hadn't read the article yet, but Kees went to buy a copy right away. After he'd read it out to the other editors in his funny Hague accent, they decided the Scouts could wait a week. We'd use the first *Otto's Slate Corner* to denounce *Privé*'s editor Henk van der Meyden and company.

We wrote a script for the show. I didn't think that was really necessary – at Radio Fed Up, I'd been working without one for years – but I held my tongue. Besides, *Slate Corner* lasted for only twenty minutes, while Radio Fed Up could be on air for hours without a script.

Introduction (Otto), record (John Denver), reading of article from Privé *(by actor, ask Jules Croiset), interview with Harry (Otto), response* Privé, *record (Jack Jersey), conclusion (Otto).*

Everything was live on air and I had to talk plainly, they said. I had had a plain pancake not long before that, which tasted very ordinary, so talking plainly meant talking the ordinary way.

'Well, I had the radio on but I didn't hear you,' Uncle Jan said on the way back. 'Or are you presenting under the pseudonym of Ad Visser?'

'We only wrote the script today.'

While I was away, things had been happening at the Blue Tit too. I smelled it as soon as I got there. Mr Elmer, the headmaster, was there and he'd brought his pipe. A meeting was in progress at the dinner table. Harry was still very angry. I interrupted Elmer, who suggested we consult a lawyer.

'Gentlemen,' I said, 'next week *Otto's Slate Corner* will be entirely devoted to the case of Harry H.'

I was sent to the dormitory straight away. I found cheeky Walter there, with the short-wave receiver that he'd got for his birthday the day before. I hadn't congratulated him, but then I hadn't known it was his birthday. He hadn't given us a treat. Walter had heard there was going to be a storm that night, so he was going to find out if it was already stormy elsewhere in the world. His radio produced a lot of noise, so I guessed that that was the case.

I couldn't sleep. Of course there were trucks on the motorway, because there were every night, but I didn't hear them. I heard the wind, a lot of wind. The Institute was battered by a hurricane, and I wondered if it was that stormy in the Veluwe. I had been planning to rub my willy, but there was too much wind, I was scared.

At three o'clock the pain tree fell down.

I was a witness because I was awake.

There's no sound in nature that's worse than a falling tree. It screamed, moaned, groaned, snapped and

78

eventually fell with a dull thud and a lot of rustling, the last goodbye of its leaves. The Blue Tit would soon be blown to the ground too, I thought.

But it wasn't. Morning broke as usual, with soggy cornflakes.

Right after breakfast I walked over to the pain tree. There it was, its trunk – of which I knew every notch – stretched out in the grass. No one would ever bump into it again. I'd never be able to climb it again. My faithful friend had been taken down. It used to wait patiently until I climbed up and sat in its branches. Now it was waiting, still patiently, for the men with the chainsaws, who arrived an hour later. The wood would be taken to the Scouts' house, to *dop dop dop, arf arf arf.* They'd use it for a campfire. The pain tree didn't deserve that, to end up as ash for those stupid *dop dop, arf arfers.* Wind, Hak explained the following morning, was the movement of air from an area with high pressure to an area with low pressure.

'So if there hadn't been any high and low pressure, the pain tree would still be standing?' I said.

'That's correct, Ottoman,' Hak said.

I had learned something new.

During the ten-thirty break, all hell broke loose at the Blue Tit. We'd secretly decided never to drink milk again. We went on strike. We wanted coffee, and fast. We formed a united front – even Edwin and cheeky Walter supported us. The staff weren't used to that. They tried to reason with us, tossing calcium and minerals into the fray, but to no avail. We stuck with our guns. When we returned to class, the tray with twelve glasses of milk on the table was already tepid. It was still there at noon, beginning to reek a little. You could smell it over Van Halen's soup-kitchen food. We were more convinced than ever we had a right to coffee. When I passed the Blackbird, Mr Willem told me Sonja was ill. She had a fever, but I was allowed to go and see her for a minute. She was in a bed in the waiting room, because that gave her privacy. I needed to ask her something really important, but I couldn't, she was too ill. I touched her face. It was warm and covered in sweat.

That day was Mr Reinier's last day. He was going on holiday. After school we celebrated with songs and guitar music by Reinier himself, and hot chocolate with skin made by Miss Letty. We sang several classics, including one by The Animals, 'Let it Be' and 'The Dutch American' with the chorus 'From front to back, from left to right'.

I sat beside Edwin, who didn't know which was left and which was right. But he couldn't help himself, because his head had got stuck during birth. I moved to the left, he to the right. And his head was very hard. We hurt ourselves so much that all festivities had to stop. The rest of the evening Edwin complained about pain in his right eye. Astonishingly, he knew it was his right eye. The staff busied themselves with cotton wool and borax lotion. At around ten o'clock he couldn't see anything any more. He had to go to the Majella. They established what had been feared, that his retina had come loose. That had happened before. I guess they'd used bad glue then. His parents were informed and were very upset. I didn't understand what all the fuss was about, it was all way over the top. What difference did it make whether you could see two per cent or nothing at all? I preferred him to see nothing, so he wouldn't bully us any more. Edwin was taken to the eye hospital in Utrecht. The Majella didn't have the right glue. Radio Fed Up broadcast a short programme before bedtime, celebrating Edwin's unexpected departure.

I had to go and see him the following day. Miss Kootje thought it was 'only fair'. I met Edwin's parents in the small room at the eye hospital.

'Look,' his mother said in a shrill, loud voice when I entered with Miss Kootje. 'Look at what you've done.'

I smirked. She had said 'look' to a blind person, at the eye hospital, of all places.

'What are you laughing about? You've blinded our son, Otto Iking. If you hadn't tripped him up, his retina wouldn't have come loose.'

Edwin enthusiastically confirmed this from his bed. I was so shocked I couldn't speak. I needed to sit down. I understood. I felt very cold all of a sudden. What an incredible, underhand bastard Edwin was! Miss Kootje didn't say anything either. She hadn't been on duty when I bumped into Edwin's head, but she came in at the end of the evening, and I'd heard Mr Reinier tell her everything. She knew I was being accused of something I hadn't done. Something I couldn't have done, even. I'd never have been able to trip up Edwin. Damn. I began to cry. No better way to suggest I was guilty. Why did I cry so easily? What had happened was irreversible. This was never going to be fine again.

'Shake hands with Edwin and tell him you're sorry,' his mother said.

She pushed me to the bed, I shook his hand and said finally, 'I didn't do it.'

Now I needed to continue. I needed to explain that we'd been singing 'The Dutch American', that we'd moved 'from front to back, from left to right', and that he didn't know which was left and which was right. It would sound so ridiculous that no one would believe me. But I couldn't think of a lie, because Miss Kootje would know that I was lying, she knew the real story. So I didn't say anything else. Edwin's parents didn't respond to my statement and asked if they could finally be on their own with their son. Shocked, I didn't say a word to Miss Kootje on the way back. How could someone deliberately let me be accused of something I hadn't done? She had betrayed me.

People were worried about me during the days that followed. Just a little. I hardly ate, I said very little and I just wanted to die, but I didn't say that. Nothing was important any more. Radio Fed Up ceased its daily broadcasts. What news could I have presented? *Eleven-year-old Otto Iking wants to die*. No one would care. Even which was to start the following week, couldn't cheer me up. Neither could Sonja. I wasn't allowed to visit her any more, she was suffering from something infectious.

They gave me double doses of Play Therapy, but that didn't work. It would only have worked if there had been enough building blocks to build a tower high enough to jump off, ending it once and for all. I went for Independence Training, fried an egg and the yolk did not break. I'd never managed that before. But I wasn't happy about it and broke it with my fork. I spent hours sitting on the fresh mound of soil where the pain tree had been. I just sat there.

Nothing and no one could cheer me up. We gained the partial right to coffee. After difficult negotiations, we'd reached a watery compromise: latte. It made no difference to me. We were even given crisps during the break. To no avail. There was a crisp factory nearby, which you could smell when the wind was right. The factory had closed down and the staff had bought all their bags of crisps. When Miss Letty was on duty, we were all given a small bag with our latte. Mr Reinier and Miss Kootje didn't allow that and the trainee had no opinion.

Two letters arrived. Van Halen brought them with the overcooked potatoes, the spinach and the hard-boiled eggs. The letters were warm and damp. One was for the staff from Edwin's parents. The other one was for me, from Edwin himself, written in Braille. It was addressed to Ottoo. Edwin wrote he was never going to return to the Institute. Then he thanked me. I couldn't believe my fingers when I read:

Thanks for triping me up, I can see much more then before.

That was it. Meanwhile, Miss Letty had read the other letter.

'You didn't trip him up, did you?' she asked.

'No.'

'But that's what his parents claim you did.'

'No, it was because of the Dutch American, you were there, weren't you?'

'They're thanking you for the fact that you tripped him up. Because if you hadn't, Edwin would never have gone to the eye hospital, and they'd never have discovered it's such an easy condition to operate on. He can see twenty per cent more now with this right eye. Tomorrow he and his parents are coming to say goodbye.'

'Children,' Edwin's mother said the following day in her shrill voice, a little less shrill this time. 'Children get up to all kinds of mischief amongst themselves.'

'Yes!' Edwin shouted.

'That's what children are like,' his mother continued. 'And it's just as well, Otto, that you're one of these naughty boys. We brought cake for you, but mind you, share it with the others.'

That was my reward, latte with cake. I was a hero. It's funny the way things can turn out.

Everyone was happy. Edwin said he was going to a rehabilitation centre, where they'd teach him to deal with all that sight. They needed to teach him how to spell too, but they probably wouldn't manage that, because that had nothing to do with being able to see. We had been relieved of the worst bully the Institute had ever known. He would never kick us again. In two weeks' time, our shins would be healed of all those sneaky kicks by the boy 'whose head had been stuck during birth', which is why he couldn't help himself. All the blind children breathed a sigh of relief.

The taxi was supposed to come at four. It was four minutes past the hour already. I felt my Braille watch nervously for the fifth time and, feeling annoyed, flipped the flap covering the hands too hard, knocking out the glass. Just then I heard the taxi drive up on the other side of the car park. It was an Audi, I recognised the loud, high sound of its engine. The taxi company was replacing all its old Mercedes with Audis. I'd been in an Audi once before. That was really cool. Audis accelerated a lot faster than the lumbering, heavy Mercedes. I stuck my watch in my trouser pocket and got in. The driver was Uncle Leo this time, Uncle Jan's brother. Luckily, he hadn't watched AVRO's *Sports Panorama*.

The AVRO janitor took me to the third floor. We took a lift, because that was better for me, he said. I didn't understand why, because there was nothing wrong with my legs. The full editorial staff of *Otto's Slate Corner* were waiting for me in recording studio 6. There was a buzz in the air, for history was about to be made – I was making my debut on national radio. I was given a festive cup of hot chocolate, which I spilled over the covers of the records we were going to play during the show. No one minded, except me. Once again they impressed upon me the importance of speaking plainly, as if I were talking into the microphone of Radio Fed Up instead of that of the honourable AVRO. Then the technician put the cleaned-up covers of John Denver and Jack Jersey on the record player, making sure they were 'all ready and set', as they said at the real radio.

'We'll start in two minutes,' Kees said.

He took me to the soundproof room, a small cubicle with carpet on the walls to make the acoustics as 'dry' as possible. It smelled of petrol. That was because of the air conditioning, Kees said. It drew its fresh air from the 's-Gravelandseweg, where the AVRO studios were. There was a window looking into the room, so the editorial staff could see me from the recording studio. I sat behind the microphone with my notes on my lap, so you wouldn't be able to hear the rustling of my fingers on the paper. My knees were trembling.

Broadcaster Lex Braamhorst announced me.

'And now I'd like to hand the floor over to my youngest colleague, Otto.'

There was the tune. I took a deep breath.

'Hello everyone, this is the first edition of *Slotto's*, I mean *Otto's Slate Corner*, a programme for children made by children, and today we're talking about a ridiculous adult mess-up to do with *Privé* magazine...'

'Cut!' Kees shouted through the intercom from behind the glass.

It had been a disaster. I'd been speaking for only seven seconds. It wasn't plain enough. How big-headed could I have been to think I could present a radio programme? I'd said '*Slotto's*', that shouldn't have happened. My notes slid off my lap. Kees came into the soundproof room and tapped me on the head.

'We're not allowed to broadcast,' he said.

'Sorry about *Slotto's*,' I said.

'It doesn't matter,' he said. 'It's not your fault. The teachers at the school in Bovensmilde have been freed.'

We went to the recording studio to listen to the extra news bulletin. We heard that Harry's and my idea had been put into practice. They'd smashed down the doors of the school. Not with Van Halen's cart, but with a tank. Stupid teachers. They always made a mess of everything. They said the seven seconds were fine, and there'd be a broadcast the following week as scheduled. They were going to call Doctor Manusama to make sure that was what really happened.

Harry was still mad at the South Moluccans and *Privé*. His parents had been accosted at least a hundred times about the interview. Everyone had read it at the hairdresser's. Harry didn't dare go home any more, he was afraid everyone in his parents' street would think him pathetic. Elmer's idea of contacting a lawyer had been put into action. Harry was convinced he and his family would win the case, because he'd recorded the interview when the editor came to their house. He'd used his memo recorder, one with really small tapes. You could put the recorder in your pocket and still record well enough for everything to be clearly audible. He'd only got it recently, and to test whether it worked, he'd turned it on. It worked. Now the lawyer could compare the tape recording with the text in *Privé*.

My Dad went for a haircut. He told me about it that evening. At the barber's he read the AVRO magazine, which had an article about *Otto's Slate Corner* and a picture of me. He said I could do with a haircut too. He'd heard the seven seconds, and thought they were great. He said he was going to come and pick me up on Friday, and that he had a surprise for me. After that happy news I went to check on Sonja. She was much better. The doctor had made a mistake. He thought she had glandular fever, which meant you're not allowed to kiss, but it was just the flu.

I had asked her about it and now she was lying naked on the blankets in the waiting room. I was as nervous as I had been in recording studio 6 that afternoon. Her tummy was soft and warm.

'Don't you want to touch my breasts?' she asked.

Ah yes, her breasts. I'd completely forgotten about them. Hak hadn't talked about them, and we didn't have any rubber models of them. They were small hills with buttons. I was done feeling them very quickly, because I was interested in something else. I got a shock when my hand got there. She had fuzz. She had an East German one. Someone knocked on the door.

'Who's there?' Sonja asked.

'Pieter!'

That was fine. He was allowed to enter, he was as blind as a bat.

'Hi!' Pieter said.

'Hi!' Sonja said.

'Shoot,' Pieter said, 'that dumb-ass Otto.'

'Otto's here too,' Sonja said.

'Oh hi, Otto. I wanted to ask you something.'

Pieter could talk to aliens with his Lenko record player. He needed to put his mouth close to the needle and shout, and they understood, answering through the speakers. He had been talking to the aliens so enthusiastically that the arm of the record player had broken. He asked if I could fix it. My hand was still on the fuzz. Sonja guided my hand to stroke it, while Pieter began some stupid story about the aliens. About what they said through his speakers. All we needed to do was say 'yes', 'no' and 'gee' once in a while.

Sonja moaned a little.

Pieter paused his story and asked if he should go and get Nurse Pauka.

No, that wouldn't be necessary. He joined me at Sonja's bedside and began to tug my arm, trying to get me to fix his record player. I let go of Sonja, I had to. I'd have to continue my investigation some other time.

There was nothing I could do to fix the arm of the record player. It was broken and needed to be taken to doctor Lenko. Pieter wouldn't be able to talk to the aliens for a while – or to play records, but he minded that much less. In the dormitory we made do with Walter's Hit Boy.

Mr de Wit, our music teacher, had important news the following morning. Leda, his guide dog, had run away. It was a disaster. De Wit lived in a normal house in the middle of Bussum and needed his dog to find his way. He'd unleashed Leda in the park, but when he'd called her, she hadn't returned. He'd called the police to report her missing, but he couldn't tell them what colour she was. Mrs de Wit didn't know either, as she was blind too. And her collar didn't have a tube with their address. The police couldn't do anything. De Wit was helpless without his dog. He'd had to take a taxi that morning.

I was much better at playing the alto flute that morning,

'All My Loving' by the Beatles in B flat. Since the dog was gone, I was no longer afraid. You couldn't blame the dog for running away, though. She probably just wanted another blind man for a change. It wasn't much fun always having De Wit at the other end of the harness. Still, I liked De Wit. We didn't always make music during his classes, he sometimes played recordings of stand-up comedy. That's what he did now, to cheer himself up a little. In that respect, stand-up comedy worked better than the Orff instruments. He put on a record by comedian Fons Jansen and laughed so loudly that he forgot about his dog for a minute. I thought it was funny too. I'd heard the sketch six times before and knew all the jokes by heart, so I laughed even before they were told. Pieter didn't, he didn't like stand-up comedy. He used to throw cushions when De Wit played stand-up comedy, which is what he was doing then. One hit my head, and I threw it back.

'Hey,' De Wit said laughing, 'who threw a cushion at my head?'

At that point Elmer came into the classroom. He'd seen what had happened, through the window in the door. He stopped Fons Jansen, grabbed me by the scruff of the neck and dragged me out of the classroom. He was furious.

'Is that funny?' he bellowed. 'How dare you, with a blind teacher!'

De Wit came out too.

'Jan,' he said, 'don't get mad. That's what we used to do ourselves with blind teachers. We even masturbated in class.'

'Don't give him any ideas,' Elmer said.

De Wit roared with laughter. He hadn't given me any ideas, because I had no idea what he was talking about. Elmer let go of me and walked away, defeated, leaving behind a cloud of fragrant pipe smoke.

'Never mind,' De Wit said, 'they don't have a clue, the sighted. Come on, let's go and listen to "The Schoolboy".'

'The Schoolboy' was a sketch by Fons Jansen. There

was a line in it that kept being repeated: '*But that's absolute crap you know!!*'

Mr Jansen had a pretty good idea what school was like.

Mr Hak was quite solemn during our next class. He said, 'The end of the year is upon us', and Harry and I would no longer be in his class the following year. We were the only ones in year six, the rest were in years four or five.

'Harry,' Hak said, 'will go to a regular school next year, that's what his parents have decided, in consultation with Mr Elmer and me.'

He probably meant a school for the sighted.

'And Otto's parents have said that they consider Ottoman ready for a place among his able-bodied peers.'

The man's language! It had probably taken him many years of regular education.

'This afternoon,' Hak continued, 'Ottoman's father will come and discuss the matter with Mr Elmer and me. My advice to his father will be favourable.'

Ah. So Hak was okay with me going to a mainstream school. But I wasn't so sure about Elmer. Perhaps the whole thing would fall through because of the cushion, or because of ringing Van Halen's doorbell and running away. If that were the case, my Dad would tell him a thing or two about sighted children. They did things that were much worse. They pushed fireworks through mailboxes. We didn't. There were no mailboxes here.

'We'll miss you,' Hak said.

Then the bell rang. While we were having our lattes and crisps – Miss Letty was on duty – they all said it'd be great if I could go to mainstream school. I had my doubts, but I didn't say anything.

After the break I was allowed to read the 'clopedia', as it was called. Hak had a Blue Band encyclopedia in his classroom. It was in Braille, and no one had ever needed to save any Blue Band wrappers for it. Braille takes a lot of space. The encyclopedia was in seven parts, called 'volumes'. I was reading Volume number 5, the letter R.

I read about rockets and rocket motors, wonderful stuff. Way better than any popular children's books.

Van Staveren talked about lightning during the double class that afternoon. Lightning with an L, which was in Volume 3. I had finished Volume 3, so I knew all about it. Lightning contained a lot of energy. One flash could provide the Institute with an entire year's worth of energy. Van Staveren somehow influenced the weather, because right then a thunderstorm broke. It wasn't too serious, with just a little thunder, but still.

At four o'clock my Dad was waiting for me in the playground. He slapped me on the back, lifted me up and gave me a kiss. He'd shaved off his beard and smelt of aftershave.

'It's done,' he said cheerfully, his voice an octave higher than usual.

I waited for the rest. It was a riddle, I guessed. It's round and hangs on the wall. Because that was all he said.

'What?' I asked.

'You'll be leaving here,' he said, 'in three weeks' time.'

'For ever?'

'Yes, for ever.'

I had done it. The highest level of education possible. No internal training as a telephonist, no Mr Splinter at the Technical School where I'd have to make abacuses, no Vocational Training School with Sonja. No, I was going to a good mainstream school in Amstelveen. My Dad was proud, he said. I thought that was rather over the top. I'd done nothing special to reach the highest level, I'd only used my braillewriter and done sums on the abacus, that was all. I needed to tell everyone at the Blue Tit, and Sonja, who was better now.

She didn't like it.

'We'll make it a success!' my Dad squeaked happily in the Saab.

He put on a Bob Dylan tape. You shouldn't do that if you want things to turn out well. According to family legend, I'd shouted, 'Can't you turn off that boring old drone?' when Dylan was played loudly in the house when I was two.

I cottoned on to it pretty early on. But it was his car and my Dad was happy, so I was too. He said that the lyrics were good, but when I asked what they were about, he was very vague. Something about freedom and oppression. I'll be able to understand Dylan next year, I thought, because I'll get English lessons at mainstream school. Perhaps he'll be more interesting then.

Vico jumped up and down like a mad dog. I'm sure he knew that I'd be living at home soon. Dogs can smell such things. *I* smelled something too, sherry. So did my Dad. He got angry and called my Mum. No answer. He ran upstairs, to their bedroom. She wasn't there. A bottle knocked over and a small pool of sherry on the table in the living room were the only proof that she had been home. That was the surprise my Dad had been talking about. She'd disappeared without a trace. The neighbours didn't know where she was either. My Dad rang some people who might know. Meanwhile, I had a cup of tea at the neighbours'. I had to call Kas and Koos's mother 'Auntie'. Kas and Koos were out, they'd gone to their electronics club. Because it was so quiet, Auntie Theresa put a record on. I didn't know what to say, and apparently neither did she. I sat uncomfortably on the unfamiliar sofa and drank my tea far too quickly. The record was *James Last In Clogs*.

After ten minutes my Dad came round to ask if I could have dinner at Auntie Theresa's. He'd managed to track down my Mum. She'd gone back to her holiday place in the Veluwe, and he was going to drive down there. I wasn't allowed to join him.

I was welcome to stay for dinner, but Auntie needed

to do some shopping first. She left me alone with James Last and the fish tank, which was no use to me, as the fish were behind glass. I did hear the little pump pumping around the water, though. Suddenly a huge beast jumped onto my lap, giving me a fright. I hadn't known it was in the room. Auntie Theresa should've told me. I'm not going to mainstream school, I thought, while the animal dug its nails through my jeans into my leg. I didn't want to live at home. You could say what you wanted about the staff of the Blue Tit, but they didn't drink sherry.

Now the animal was caught in my shirt. I hoped it wasn't some dangerous predator.

My Dad was a dick, I thought suddenly. I hadn't even been allowed to be with him when he was calling people to find out where my Mum was. I hadn't been allowed to go with him in the Saab to pick her up. He'd just left me behind. And why did no one ever ask me whether I wanted to go to mainstream school?

The animal was now sitting on my neck, sniffing my hair.

Then Kas and Koos got back from the electronics club.

'Hey,' they said in unison, 'get off, stupid cat!'

Kas and Koos both had Philips construction kits. You could use them to build instruments that really worked. That day they'd built a light detector at the club, especially for me. The light detector beeped when light shone on the LDR, they explained like smarty-pants who read children's science magazines. The LDR was a light-dependent resistor. The more light on the LDR, the higher the beep. That way I'd be able to hear the sun come up, they said. An interesting invention. They said I could test the machine the next morning. Then we climbed onto the kitchen worktop, as close to the extractor fan as possible, which we put on the highest setting, and had a smoke. Tigger, the cat, kept jumping onto the worktop, but was roughly removed each time. I still couldn't inhale. No sooner had we put out our cigarettes under the tap and thrown them in the bin than

Auntie Theresa came back.

'What's that smell?' she asked.

'Ah,' said Kas, 'that's what we were wondering too, so we switched on the extractor fan.'

'No, no,' she said, raising her voice, 'it's smoke. Who's been smoking?'

I expected them to say it was me, but they didn't.

'We did,' they said together.

They often said things at the same time, but they were twins.

'I had one too,' I said to support them.

She was very angry and said she'd tell Uncle Sjoerd the minute he came home. He'd know what to do with boys like that. Five minutes later he was there. Whistling, he flung his bag down.

'Hi there, everyone,' he said when he walked into the room. But his mood changed quickly and his lecture for Kas and Koos ended with, 'No pocket money next week!'

There was a very long silence. I could only hear the pump in the fish tank, and Tigger, who miaowed softly. It sounded like, 'Don't blame *me*, I tried to stop them.'

We had to start again from scratch. Someone put on *James Last In Clogs*, but no one spoke. We didn't know what to say. And when we did say something, it sounded odd and made no sense. The lecture rang in our ears. But then Uncle Sjoerd went upstairs to change and Auntie Theresa went off to cook. Relieved, we inhaled the smells of the cooking and Kas put on Supertramp.

'What's this?' Kas asked when we were at table.

'It's cheese fondue,' Auntie Theresa said.

'Yuk, I don't like these strings.'

He made a sound like he was going to throw up.

'Don't make such a fuss,' his mother said. 'Just eat!'

'Why did you cook this?' he asked.

'Because Otto's here for dinner,' she said. 'His family likes cheese fondue.'

We did have cheese fondue once in a while, but this one

94

was much saltier and stringier. Sweet Auntie Theresa. She was trying to make me feel as comfortable as she could. Auntie Theresa wanted to do everything my Mum did. She really looked up to my Mum. But she had no idea about my Mum, she didn't know about the drinking, of course. No, she was away on holiday for a few weeks, spoiling herself. If only Auntie Theresa could do that, but she had children at home, and a husband who couldn't do anything by himself.

They all thought the fondue was strange. I felt embarrassed, because it had been cooked especially for me, and the saltiness was making me sweat.

'Thanks for dinner,' I said to Auntie Theresa when we were done. The fondue wasn't finished, but I couldn't eat any more.

'You need to say it properly,' Kas whispered. '*Thank you.*'

'No,' his mother said. 'You need to, but Otto doesn't. They don't do that at his house.'

I felt even more embarrassed. Uncle Sjoerd said, 'I hope you've enjoyed your meal,' and we were allowed to leave the table. They watched a film. Kas read out the subtitles, but it wasn't any fun. They didn't talk much in that film. At ten o'clock my parents still hadn't arrived. The boys needed to go to bed, but because I was there, they were allowed to stay up. They hoped my parents would never come back. Uncle Sjoerd had just started to blow up an airbed for me when I heard the Saab.

'It didn't work,' my Dad said.

We were sitting in the darkroom. He'd switched on the light, I could hear it in his voice. We might as well have stayed downstairs.

He said, 'I expected everything to go well when you came, but she can't handle it apparently. I don't know. I don't know.'

He said it five more times.

'What do we do now?' he asked.

I didn't say anything, I didn't know. It was all my fault. She couldn't handle me coming home.

'You'd better go to bed,' he said.

I did, setting my alarm for five o'clock, which I thought would be early enough to hear the sun come up with Kas and Koos's apparatus. I fell asleep during 'Mr Tambourine Man'.

At five o'clock sharp I switched on Kas and Koos's machine, and turned up the volume as high as it would go. Then I lay down to wait for the sun. At nine o'clock I was woken by my Dad, who came to bring me some rusks and tea.

'Did the sun come up?' I asked.

'Sure, it's bright and sunny outside. If you wanted to hear the sun, you should've opened the curtains.'

Of course. I'd try again tomorrow. Surely the sun would come up again. My Dad seemed to have forgotten all about the previous day's misery. We took the tandem to a fun fair in Amsterdam. I loved the dodgem cars best, especially when my Dad did the driving. When I was at the wheel, we bumped into others far too often, slowing us down too much. We had chips and *poffertjes*, miniature pancakes. In the evening there was football on the telly. As usual, my Dad provided the commentary, but no one scored.

On Sunday I forgot to set my alarm to hear the sun come up. We went to visit Granny in Hillegom, taking the train because the Saab wouldn't start. Granny picked us up from the station in her Daf. She talked so much that she didn't notice she'd driven through red lights. At least, that's what my Dad said. She didn't believe him, but I did.

During the war people hid in a cupboard in Granny's house. I knew where to find it and, when I was at my Granny's, I always spent an hour or so in there. Granny would look for me and could never find me. But this time the hiding place was taken, my cousin Petra was already hiding there. So I went to the attic. The attic was full of apples, because my grandmother had an apple tree in the garden. I was supposed to turn them over, but I kept forgetting which ones I'd already turned. There was a stuffed horse there too, who loved the apples. We were not allowed to sit on the horse, because it might break, but I did anyway and it didn't. I made two holes in it when I dug my heels into it, but it went like the wind. I galloped across all the rooftops of Hillegom. Downstairs, I found Uncle Bob, my Dad's brother, in the living room. Uncle Bob could fly a private plane, and I was invited to go with him during the summer holiday. We had dinner at Granny's too. It was a little like the food at the Institute. No, slightly better. Then we took a taxi to the station. When we were on the train, my Dad told me that he didn't dare to go in a car my Granny was driving any more.

On Monday morning the Saab suddenly started again and there was a traffic jam. That didn't happen very often, but an LPG tanker had fallen over, and that was very dangerous. I arrived at the Institute twenty minutes late. I wished there were toppled LPG tankers more often. When we were parking the car, I told my Dad that I didn't want to go to mainstream school as long as things were bad at home with Mum. He didn't say anything.

Things were different in class now that I knew I'd be leaving. I wondered whether anything I was doing was really necessary. Primary school was over after all, no one could change that. I moved some beads around on the abacus, did some division, added and subtracted, but it was no use. Hak noticed and took me to his office.

'Well,' he said, blowing smoke, 'does Ottoman not feel like going to mainstream school?'

'I do.'

'You look worried.'

My Dad had told me not to say anything about my Mum's drinking. Of course I wouldn't. Hak was just talking. He said he thought I was afraid of mainstream school. Which was logical, because it'd be a big change

97

for me. The world of the able-bodied could be tough. This lasted another two cigarettes. Then he'd smoked enough and we went back to the classroom.

Fortunately our next class was with Mr de Wit. No stand-up comedians this time, but making music in a trio, with De Wit, and Marc on the recorder. When you play it well, it sounds like an organ. We played the *Water Music* by Handel. It immediately began to rain outside. During the break we decided Radio Fed Up would discuss the Harry H case. Harry had brought the tape with the interview with *Privé*, which we would broadcast so everyone could hear the actual interview. After that, I'd play the *Water Music*. I had a memo tape recorder myself now, and I'd recorded the trio. This varied programme was to be concluded with 'The Schoolboy' by Fons Jansen. I'd borrowed the tape from Mr de Wit.

Mr Mooyman, our gymnastics teacher, had us do something new after the break: goal ball. We were eight in all, so were divided into two parties of four, standing opposite each other on the walking track close to the wall on the short ends of the gym. Then we rolled the heavy rubber ball with the bells across. If you didn't play it close to the ground, you had to sit on the bench beside Mooyman for a while, as punishment. The ball wasn't to touch the wall behind us, because if it did the opponents got a point. But the ball hardly even reached our opponents – it usually hit the bench that Mooyman was sitting on. After fifty minutes of determined rolling, the score was still 0-0. No penalties either, unfortunately.

After that was Independence Training. For me, at least. I asked if I could make cheese fondue, but there was no wine and I didn't fancy making cheese fondue with lemonade, so I made tea instead. I'd known how to do that for ages, but I couldn't think of anything else (I was supposed to think of something myself).

A new kindergarten was being built on the field in front of the Blue Tit. When I was testing the Jostikit for the evening broadcast during our lunch break, I heard myself on the builders' radio. I said that there was beer for them at the Blue Tit. They cheered and a minute later I heard an angry exchange between some of them and Mr Reinier. He came to me a few minutes later, furious, to tell me that I shouldn't say such things on the radio. It was really easy to wind him up.

Since the weather was good for once, lunch was to be outside. As far as I know, that was the only time ever. The tables with greasy tablecloths were hauled outside by far too many people, breaking one of the windows in the back door, but that didn't matter. It wasn't the first time. Actually, it happened so often that the lower panes had already been replaced with wooden boards. We didn't eat much, because we thought there was a wasp. Mr Reinier swore there wasn't one, but no one believed him and we flailed about wildly. We lifted the tables up again and took them back inside. Then I was stung on my lip. So there had been a wasp after all, one that had fled inside because all the crazy blind kids were making such a din outside. I could understand that, but why did he have to pick me? I was the only one who was not afraid – even Harry was terrified. Ha, Harry, scared of a little wasp. It hurt, but some vinegar quickly dulled the pain. I talked funny with my swollen lip, but I didn't have to say anything for the rest of the afternoon.

Van Staveren, our physics teacher, talked for two hours about radio waves. About the difference between AM and FM waves. He said that FM waves could be received in space. Which meant that even in space you could listen to Radio Fed Up. So that's why you could hear the editor of *Privé* talking in space that evening, to Harry, to his sister and to his parents. And my alto flute could be heard on Uranus. That night I dreamt about mainstream school. They were playing tag, and I was always It.

The following morning I returned the Fons Jansen tape to De Wit. Leda was back, and she made sure I noticed. She bit into my trouser leg and dragged me across the whole classroom, knocking over several Orff instruments that crashed to the floor. Great guide dog, Leda. De Wit intervened. Leda had been in the park all that time, he told us, and had been returned to him by one of his neighbours. She was still a little aggressive because she hadn't eaten for so long. I let De Wit feel my torn trouser leg. He said he'd find out what a new pair of trousers cost and pay me the next day.

Harry and I had nothing left to do in Mr Hak's class. We'd finished reading our books, and we didn't need to take any exams. We were done with primary school and that was that. Using the Braille folding ruler I measured the length of the corridor: it was 20.07 yards long. Good to know! I planted rose geranium cuttings, moved some beads on the abacus, and read the 'clopedia' (having reached S for 'starting motor'). I wasn't bored. I was never bored in class. I sat for hours listening to the others, who still had lots to learn. I just sat there and didn't even pretend to be doing very much.

Hak was fine with that. Once in a while he made me do little chores, like taking his coffee cup back to the kitchen downstairs to be washed. Totally pointless. But then he thought of something better to do. He sent me to help out Mr Soeters.

Mr Soeters ran the library on the top floor of the main building. It was a maze of bookcases with hundreds of yards of Braille books. If anyone needed a book, they called Soeters. He would locate it, put it in the book lift and send it down. Several teachers had complained that sometimes it took too long for the books to arrive, so someone had decided the books needed to be catalogued. Soeters didn't like the plan, particularly because he hadn't been consulted. But I thought it was a good idea, because I was allowed to help him. Together we scanned the bookcases

– me first, then Soeters, dragging his heavy braillewriter along. I read out the numbers written in Braille on the spines of the books. Soeters wrote them down. Then I opened the book, read out the title and told him how many volumes it consisted of. *War and Peace* by Tolstoy was 55 volumes, and Volumes 33 and 48 were missing. They had to be elsewhere in the library. Many other books also had several volumes missing. It was one huge literary mess up there. I found Volume 33 of *War and Peace* between Volumes 2 and 3 of *Mein Kampf*, which some blind Nazi had Braille-ified. Volume 48 stayed lost until it was found by chance years later, in a fat critic's private archive. The cataloguing took a very long time, not least because I began to read all the books I came across. I didn't know what was happening to me. I was used to Hak's ration of one book a week. It was unbelievable, there were so many books to read! Soeters liked having me there. He'd always been alone on the top floor. Once they'd accidentally locked him in, but he hadn't minded very much. He'd listened to a radio play called *Looking for the Left Leg* all night. The leg was found at five in the morning.

Between Volume 6 of *The Stone Bridal Bed* and Volume 2 of *Beyond Sleep* I found Piet Paaltjens, or at least part of *Sobs and Bitter Grins*. I read 'The Suicide' and immediately decided to steal it. I found Volume 2 among the *Little Golden Books*, which filled more than three yards of bookshelves. Before I left, I put Paaltjens in the book lift and pressed the button for the ground floor. I was planning to learn all his poems by heart.

I really liked the smell of the library. Not many people know the smell of old, damp Braille paper with dots flattened by numerous fingers, but believe me, it's way better than spring blossom. Soeters had done really well for himself. If he ever left, I wanted his job.

Soeters had an interesting hobby. He collected sounds. Every morning when I arrived on the top floor, I heard something different. One time it was a French steam train from 1913, another time a napalm bombardment or a waterfall in Chile. Soeters had built an impressive archive over the years, even the BBC would have had a hard time beating it. You name it, he had it, from the detonation of the first H-bomb to the crying of a baby girl. From shooting Nazis to shooting Stasis, which sounded very similar. From two high-heeled ladies to a trotting horse – they too were difficult to tell apart. From a cart on a dirt track to the rush hour on the Champs-Élysées – in both cases traffic was slow.

Soeters had placed speakers in different places among the bookcases filled with Braille books. We did our cataloguing to sounds of a sunrise in the tropical rainforest or a sunset in the Schwarzwald. Nature was immune to the ravages of humanity on that floor. All plants and animals remained as unspoiled as they had been when they were recorded.

I wanted to stay in the library until I had absorbed every sound Soeters had collected. I wanted all dots of all Braille books to pass through my hands. But that was impossible. After a week in the world of Mr Soeters, Hak ordered me back to the classroom. Soeters and I weren't done yet, not by far. If anything, the mess was even bigger than before I joined him.

Everything outside the library suddenly seemed incredibly dull. Hak had thought of yet another chore: I was to rewrite the illegible Braille dots in the books for the little ones. There was nothing happening at the Blue Tit either, so the Radio Fed Up broadcasts were almost entirely music. The only thing worth mentioning was Harry's success. His family had won the court case against *Privé*. They were to be paid damages, which Harry could use to buy a drum kit. Soon the entire neighbourhood would enjoy the fruits of the injustice done to him.

It was a shame they'd won the court case, because even though the Radio Fed Up broadcast had been a success, apparently we couldn't talk about Harry on the *Slate*

Corner any more.

'Well,' said Kees from the AVRO over the telephone, 'then we'll just do the Scout issue, simple enough.'

Sure enough it took very little effort to fill twenty minutes slating the Scouts. We did it the following day, enthusiastically. I was so happy to be able to talk into a microphone again that I forgot my text and launched into a long rant about the Scouts that was only stopped by switching off my mike. We annihilated those pathetic *dop dop arfers*, we'd wiped the floor with them. There were three phone calls from angry adults after that, with one adult cancelling his subscription to the AVRO. It was my fault, but the editorial staff loved what I did. After the show there was a little party in the AVRO studio restaurant to which I was also invited. Someone handed out chocolates, and I accidentally put one with wrapper and all into my mouth. Everyone noticed and laughed. I wanted to leave.

When I was back at the Blue Tit I asked Mr Reinier if he'd be willing to subscribe to the AVRO, so the number of subscribers would stay the same. But he said, 'No, I've already got a subscription to the TROS broadcasting corporation.'

God, Sonja was really happy. Someone being so happy was annoying. At first I thought it was to do with my radio performance, but she didn't even listen to it.

'Mainstream school,' she kept yelling, 'mainstream school!'

How irritating. After five minutes of her screaming and jumping up and down I discovered why she was so excited about mainstream school. She too would go the following year. She was ready for it, the Institute had decided, because she'd made such a grown-up impression at the Vocational Training School or something. Well, maybe she did at the Vocational Training School, but she sure as heck wasn't now. Her foster parents had accepted the advice, and now she was to go to year one of mainstream secondary school. She was repeating the year on purpose to get used to the school.

What nonsense! How could the Institute have changed its mind so quickly? Until very recently there was no way she'd have been allowed to go to mainstream school. If that was how they treated their pupils, they could call my Dad to say they'd decided I wasn't ready to go to mainstream school after all. They were quite capable of that.

Soeters explained when I was sent to the library one more time to return some novels. They simply had too few students at the Vocational Training School and needed to get rid of a teacher. They'd made a new teaching schedule, and because Sonja was the only one in year two of secondary school the next year, they'd decided to abolish year two. That's how things worked. They're just messing around, Soeters said, and that's why he also messed around. He wasn't going to set up an entire catalogue system for the one and a half blind people who borrowed three books a year. So he played me an episode of *Looking for the Left Leg*.

It struck me that the staff behaved rather oddly towards me. They were much nicer to me than usual. They'd suddenly begun to touch me, stroke my hair and pinch my cheeks. I let them. I sort of liked it, but I didn't trust them. They sounded a little sad when they said something to me. No, not sad, but as if they were sorry for me. It had already been going on for three days. I didn't ask any questions, I wanted to keep it that way, even though they didn't mean it.

And then, suddenly, my Dad appeared. He needed to talk to me. He took me upstairs, to the small waiting room. We sat down on the bed and he began to talk very slowly.

'Your mother,' he said.

He stopped. She was dead.

'Mum has been admitted to a psychiatric clinic because she's very confused.'

I was immensely relieved.

'And Dad,' he continued – he childishly called himself Dad – 'Dad's going to America for a year.'

Sure, America, why not? It was him who was confused. He couldn't go. The summer holidays were about to start, I was going to be at home, and after that I was going to mainstream school.

'I've been offered a placement with a newspaper. An opportunity I can't afford to pass up.' He tried to sound convincing, but his squeaky voice let him down. There was a long silence.

He sighed.

I sighed.

He sighed again. I sighed again.

I heard the children shouting outside. Downstairs, someone was whistling a tune. An aeroplane flew overhead and a gust of warm wind came through the open window. Mr Reinier drove off on his moped. Someone switched on the radio in the dormitory. Trucks whizzed along the motorway.

'I'm leaving next week.'

'But what about me?' I asked.

'You can stay at Granny's during the holidays and the neighbours are going to Luxembourg for three weeks. You can go with them. You'd like that, wouldn't you, with Koos and Kas?'

'And after the holidays?'

'You'll come back here and go to the Vocational Training School. So you'll be with Sonja after all.'

'But Sonja's leaving,' I said.

He didn't hear. He didn't respond, at least. I was confused.

'So when will you come back?' I asked.

'Next year.'

'And what about Mum?'

'It's better for me,' he said, 'not to see Mum any more. I can't help her any longer. I've done what I can, it's up to other people now. Right, I'll be off. I won't see you for a while, but I'll send you tapes from America. I'll record letters on them. I'll leave my address with the staff, so you can send something back.'

This was *not* my Dad. Everything would be all right. I didn't have to go to Luxembourg with the neighbours. After all, I was going to mainstream school.

'Next week,' he said, 'you'll be picked up by Uncle Sjoerd.'

He got up and so did I. I smelled his sweat. He was breathing quickly through his nose. He walked down the stairs and I followed. He crossed the living room without greeting anyone. No one said anything to him. Outside he said, 'Bye,' and then walked away quickly. I ran after him. I tripped over the sandpit and hit my head on the wooden cover. He must have heard, but he didn't come back. That was my Dad. Traitor. Sitting on the cover of the sandpit, I heard the Saab drive off, with Dylan singing:

How does it feel
to be on your own
to be without a home
like a rolling stone.

I didn't understand the English words, but I got the picture. Blood and tears mingled on my face and the sandpit cover shook with my sobs. It started to rain, but I didn't care. I was going to sit there until I'd bled dry or cried myself to death.

At the clinic, Nurse Pauka stitched up my head wound. Miss Letty, who'd found me on the cover of the sandpit, was suddenly genuinely nice. When we walked back to the Blue Tit, she said my Dad probably wouldn't go to America. We'd talk to him and he'd realise he couldn't do that, because he had such a sweet son. I didn't want to contradict her. My fate was sealed: the Vocational Training School without Sonja, without Harry and without my parents. Things would never be okay again. I'd never see either of my parents ever again. My Mum couldn't help being confused, it was my fault. She couldn't stand me being at home, it made her drink. But my Dad, who simply took off to America, who was ready to hand me over to the neighbours, to Auntie Theresa and Uncle Sjoerd, who always had to be there for me when my Dad wasn't – my Dad had betrayed and abandoned me. He was a cowardly, egotistical son of a bitch who stank of sweat and had a squeaky voice. I wanted to die, just like the suicide Piet Paaltjens had written about, but I had no tie to tie myself up with. I threw up all my food, lay down on my bed and stopped eating, which I'd continue to do until I was dead. It'd be my Dad's fault.

A man came to talk to me. He was a social worker. I didn't need to say anything if I didn't want to, he said. So I didn't say anything. But he still stayed for some time and asked me questions. Which I didn't answer, because I didn't have to say anything. Miss Letty came to beg me to please have a rusk with a slice of roast beef. I finally had one on day three. I couldn't stand it any more, I was so hungry, I had to eat.

Sonja came to see me too, but it left me cold. She was going away, I had to stay at the Institute. It was over

107

between us. Soeters sent me a book through someone, but I didn't have the energy to move my hands over the paper. They tried to call my Dad, but couldn't get hold of him.

Then I abandoned my protest. I didn't want to die without my Dad knowing, because then I'd have died in vain. I got up and ate a lot of Kingcorn with sandwich spread. Miss Letty was relieved. I got a postcard from my Mum saying she was allowed to leave the clinic next week.

But the following day I received a letter from the head of the department where she was being treated, saying that was not the case. He wrote that they read all the outgoing patients' mail. Her situation was serious. She was a danger to her surroundings and to herself – she'd tried to commit suicide. I wondered how she'd done that. Had she used a tie? It didn't say. I could ask her, I was going to see her at her special request.

She was called Mrs Iking and she lived in room 712 at the Robin Pavilion. When I entered with Miss Letty, her hug nearly crushed me to a pulp.

'That girl can go,' she shouted, 'right away!'

Miss Letty left.

When we'd walked from the car to the Robin, I'd heard people shout and scream all around me, just like at the Institute, only here there were adults. I could still hear them in my Mum's room, even with the door and all the windows closed.

'Don't worry about them,' Mrs Iking said, 'those are the crazies.'

'Are you crazy too?' I asked.

'No, I'm completely normal, I'm leaving here tomorrow. They can all go to hell. I'm going home to look after you and we'll go on holiday to America, and at the end of the summer I'm going to set up my own fashion school in Amsterdam. A hundred and fifty people have signed up already, so I'll have to draw up waiting lists, because I'm sure you'll understand that I won't be able to teach all those people myself. And once the school is up and running, I'll hire lots of top teachers. The school will be a centre of international fashion. And you, you'll become a brilliant scientist. You'll have your sight back in two months' time and nothing will be able to stop you. Together, we'll be in all the magazines – the successful mother and son from the Princess Margriet Park in Amstelveen. But we won't be living there any more, of course, in that miserable bourgeois place. And your father is a prick.'

I'm not sure what the latter had to do with it, but she was right about him.

'I just need a nice guy,' she continued. 'There's a doctor here whom I wouldn't mind seeing. He could support me financially while I'm setting up my fashion school.'

I didn't answer and I didn't need to, because she just kept going. She had lots more plans. She was going to do a PhD, she was going to be a candidate for Culture Secretary and she was going to become the chairwoman of the World Wildlife Fund.

After an hour I was finally allowed to leave. My Mum was angry I had to go, but those were the Robin's rules. Great rules.

When I returned to the Blue Tit, Sonja was waiting for me. She was annoyingly happy again. I had to go with her, she said, to the Blackbird. She wouldn't say why. I didn't want to go, but she insisted, so in the end I did. Her foster parents were there, at the Blackbird. They knew all about me, and so did Sonja. They must have heard from the staff, because *I* certainly didn't tell Sonja. I wished the staff would keep their mouths shut. My misery was nobody else's business. But they were really nice, Sonja's foster parents, and they made me an offer. If I wanted – I needed to tell them right away if I didn't – I could spend the entire summer holiday with them. They were going to Luxembourg, and if the car could hold three people, it could hold four, they said. I didn't believe it. I didn't believe anyone any more. But they kept repeating themselves, and they were so nice, and Sonja was so happy about it. (They didn't tell me this, she did.) She began to jump up and down again, and suddenly I didn't think all that happiness was irritating any more. I had to believe. I too began to jump up and down and be happy. Great! I wouldn't go to Luxembourg with the neighbours, but I'd still go to Luxembourg! I just hoped we wouldn't bump into the neighbours, because Luxembourg wasn't very large and they might take me with them if we did.

From then on, things happened really quickly. The last few days of school were over before I knew it. I played the *Water Music* on my alto flute one more time, and I knew I'd never perform better than that. I did everything Hak told me to. I took away his empty cups, planted more cuttings, fixed books for the little ones and measured the corridor again with the Braille folding ruler. It was now 20.1 yards. I must have got it wrong the previous time. I didn't say goodbye to anyone, just to Harry, whom I wouldn't see the following year. It wasn't a big thing, we just said, 'Well, bye,' and that was it. Then Sonja, her foster parents and I got into their Audi. We drove away, blowing the horn, the tyres screeching as we turned the corner, out of the car park.

After a week, I called Sonja's foster parents Mum and Dad, just like she did. It was no effort at all.

I still do.

He went back once, to the Institute, to execute a secret mission. His new parents dropped him off. He walked to Mr Reinier's moped armed with the siphon bucket that was still stored with the cleaning things at the Blue Tit. He filled the bucket to the brim. Then he slowly walked around the Institute, sprinkling everything he came across with petrol. When he was done, he lit a Camel. Satisfied, he inhaled the smoke – he could finally inhale. Then he threw the cigarette butt onto the trail of petrol. He felt the heat immediately. The flames spread quickly in the strong wind. It got hotter and hotter when the flames reached the rhododendrons and crept from the primary school to the lodgings. Up they went in flames, the Blue Tit, the Blackbird, the Finch and the Wagtail. He heard them scream in pain. Piss Pieter shouted, 'Dumb-ass Otto' before the hungry flames consumed him. Marga repeated what he said, but then she too was consumed by the devastating fire. Mr Reinier sang 'The House of the Rising Sun' one more time, but it didn't help. Miss Kootje entered the room with soggy cornflakes. No one would ever taste them again. Walter began a sermon about hell and damnation, and was right in the middle of it before he realised what was happening. Super blind Harry couldn't escape either. The heat was so intense that his glass eyeballs cracked.

Elmer walked up to the arsonist and shouted, 'Is that fun?'

'Yes, Mr Elmer,' he said. 'This is fun.'

Mooyman, Van Halen, Hak, De Wit, Miss Trudy who taught Play Therapy – everyone, even Soeters – had to die. He was sorry about Soeters, but he wouldn't mind. Soeters never minded anything. The log cabin, the seesaw, the main building, the clinic, the kitchen, the linen-room, the Beat Cellar for the older blind kids, where they drank beer and shagged, the printing office, even the reception and Van Halen's cart turned to ashes in the all-consuming sea of fire.

While Leda barked for the very last time, he walked

past the reception, through the gate, turned right, walked along the service road, crossed the service road at the motorway flyover, crossed the flyover and, turning left, arrived at the petrol pump. He walked without a stick, he didn't need one any more, he knew the route by heart. He bought a new packet and lit a fresh Camel while he waited.

The tyres screeched when his new parents, Sonja and he drove off for the very last time – on their way to mainstream school. Smoke and ashes were all that remained of the Institute but whether that smoke was black, he couldn't tell.

THE AUTHOR

Vincent Bijlo is a Dutch stand-up comedian,
columnist, musician and author. Many appearances
on TV, radio and in the theatre have made him
a household name in the Netherlands.

He studied Dutch language and literature at the University
of Utrecht, and in 1988 he won the public's prize and the
best personality prize at the Cabaret Festival in Leiden.

This was the start of Bijlo's successful career as a stand-
up comedian. He has written many theatre shows, from
Made in Braille in 1989 to his current tour of *Het nieuwe
nu* (*The New Present*). In 2016/17, he appears together
with The Rosettis, of which his wife Mariska Reijmerink
is a member, in *Op Woeste Hoogte* (*Wuthering Heights*),
a musical theatre production about the Brontë family.

Vincent is a well-known radio presenter and columnist
for one of the Dutch national newspapers.

Dutch publishing house De Arbeiderspers published his
four novels: *Het instituut* in 1998, *Achttienhoog* in 2001, *De
woordvoerder* in 2003 and *De Ottomaanse herder* in 2009.

Vincent Bijlo was born blind.

www.vincentbijlo.com

THE TRANSLATOR

Susan Ridder studied at the universities of Utrecht, Glasgow and Exeter and is a certified translator. She translates fiction, non-fiction and poetry from Dutch to English and from English to Dutch.

Susan works with several of the leading publishing houses including De Arbeiderspers, JM Meulenhoff, De Geus and Weidenfeld & Nicholson.

Holland Park Press is a unique publishing initiative. Its aim is to promote poetry and literary fiction, and discover new writers. It specializes in contemporary English fiction and poetry, and translations of Dutch classics. It also gives contemporary Dutch writers the opportunity to be published in Dutch and English.

To

- Learn more about Vincent Bijlo
- Discover other interesting books
- Read our unique Anglo-Dutch magazine
- Find out how to submit your manuscript
- Take part in one of our competitions

Visit www.hollandparkpress.co.uk

Bookshop: http://www.hollandparkpress.co.uk/books.php

Holland Park Press in the social media:

http://www.twitter.com/HollandParkPres
http://www.facebook.com/HollandParkPress
https://www.linkedin.com/company/holland-park-press
http://www.youtube.com/user/HollandParkPress